**The next n**

To Osmond Wright:

*Ecclesiastes 12:14. For God shall bring every work into judgment, with every secret thing, whether it be good, or whether it be evil.*

Your secrets are no longer safe, Osmond. His judgment is nearer than you think and I have appointed myself His Executioner here on earth. Be prepared to pay or forfeit all.

                                          –One who knows

The author snickered as the gray watermark bond slipped from the roller with a whoosh. Osmond Wright would finally begin to understand what was in store for him.

Hands covered by gloves, the author folded the note and slipped it into an envelope.

# ABOUT THE AUTHOR

Patricia Rosemoor began creating romantic fantasies as a child, never guessing that someday she would be writing for Harlequin Books. Although writing demands a lot of time, Patricia can't think of another profession that would allow her to explore so many intriguing settings and subjects. She thinks of each new idea as a challenge, creating a story that will fascinate her readers.

## Books by Patricia Rosemoor

### HARLEQUIN INTRIGUE

### HARLEQUIN SUPERROMANCE

Don't miss any of our special offers. Write to us at the following address for information on our newest releases.

Harlequin Reader Service
901 Fuhrmann Blvd., P.O. Box 1397, Buffalo, NY 14240
Canadian address: P.O. Box 603,
Fort Erie, Ont. L2A 5X3

# Do Unto Others

**Patricia Rosemoor**

*Harlequin Books*

TORONTO • NEW YORK • LONDON
AMSTERDAM • PARIS • SYDNEY • HAMBURG
STOCKHOLM • ATHENS • TOKYO • MILAN

To Linda,
for holding my hand
through this one . . .
and to Chevi,
for the cement goose

Harlequin Intrigue edition published May 1989

ISBN 0-373-22113-4

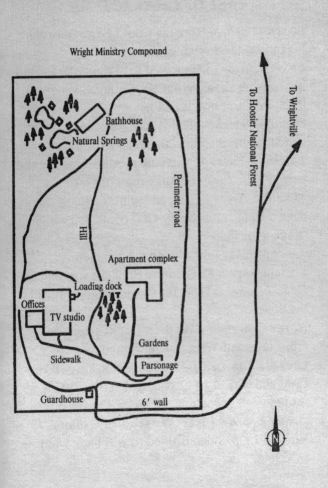

Wright Ministry Compound

Bathhouse

Natural Springs

Perimeter road

Hill

Apartment complex

Loading dock

Offices

TV studio

Gardens

Sidewalk

Parsonage

Guardhouse

6' wall

To Hoosier National Forest

To Wrightville

N

# CAST OF CHARACTERS

*Logan Wright*—How far would he go to protect his father, the televangelist?

*Bliss Griffith*—She arrived in Wrightville to find her missing sister. What she found was more than she had bargained for.

*Osmond Wright*—To his followers, he was a savior; to his enemies, the devil in disguise.

*Lurlene Wright*—Quiet and modest; was she the perfect wife for a dynamic man of God?

*Melody Sawyer*—She had stumbled upon the deadly note . . . and only God could answer her prayers for help.

*Joelle Mackey*—Flashy and outspoken, Lurlene's sister knew more than she was telling.

*Dean Mackey*—How far would he go to fulfill his lifelong obsession?

*Roger Cahnman*—He didn't want salvation from Osmond Wright—he wanted revenge.

*Gregory Townsend*—No one dared suspect the financial officer of having stolen the missing money.

*Arden Heath*—Rival evangelist of Osmond Wright, he was determined to win back what he'd lost.

# *Prologue*

The scent of roses threatening to choke her, Melody Sawyer edged away from the scene in the garden, almost panicking when her lace-trimmed dress caught on a bush. She tugged at the material and gasped with relief when it ripped free of the thorns. Then she ran away from the parsonage and across the moonlit compound as if her life depended on her undetected escape.

Her heart raced as fast as her feet. She didn't stop to see if anyone followed but pressed on, calling up every ounce of reserve energy. Panting by the time she reached the apartment complex, she flung open the outer door. The stairway beckoned, a quicker route than the elevator. She took the steps two at a time until she reached her third-floor apartment.

Once inside, Melody leaned against the closed door for a moment and listened. No sound of pounding feet could be heard through the halls.

"Thank you, Lord," she whispered.

She pulled the folded piece of dove-gray paper from her pocket. Instinctively she moved through the small apartment, looking for a place to hide the evidence. In the bedroom, her gaze fell on her Bible. How fitting. She even found the appropriate verse before wedging the note tightly between the pages. Then she opened the night-stand drawer and placed the Bible inside. Her hands were shaking as she slid the drawer closed.

She needed someone to talk to.

Needed to be rescued. *Again.*

This time was different, Melody reassured herself. Still, tears welled in her eyes as she glanced at the clock. The blue numbers glowed in the dimly lit room: 2:23 a.m. She hesitated only a second before dialing. She counted the rings. One. Two. Three. Halfway through the fourth, the receiver lifted on the other end.

"Hello, are you there?" Melody whispered.

A scrabbling sound was followed by an impatient, "This had better be important."

"I . . . I think I'm in trouble."

"Melody?"

"Sorry if I woke you, but I didn't know what else to do."

"Do about what?"

"I found something I shouldn't have. Instead of getting rid of it and minding my own business, I decided to investigate. . . ."

"Wait a minute. You're going too fast. What did you find?"

Before Melody could answer, she sensed a presence behind her. Whipping around, she spotted him looming in the doorway, large and threatening. The telephone dropped from her suddenly nerveless fingers.

"Melody?" The disembodied voice came from the discarded receiver.

Melody forced herself to smile at the intruder. "You startled me."

"Melody! What's going on?" came the distant shout. "Who's there?"

The man disconnected the line and the phone went dead. Melody took a step back. Her heart was pounding so hard that she swore she could hear its rush in her ears.

"You didn't answer me," she said with false bravado. "It's awfully late."

She told herself to keep her head, but how could she when his threatening expression made her knees weak?

"You know why I'm here."

Of course she did. He must have spotted her when she'd been playing amateur detective. Why hadn't she stayed in her apartment and minded her own business?

He flipped on the television. So that the noise would cover her screams? Melody wondered as she glanced at the program. Ironically Congregation of the Lord Network was rerunning *An Hour with Osmond Wright*.

She took another step back—right into a corner. Right into his hands—strong, threatening ones that were coming for her throat.

"No, don't! I promise I won't tell!"

"I know you won't."

"Fear you not." The silver-haired televangelist's voice boomed rich and full from the television. "Stand still and see the salvation of the Lord, which he will show to you today."

Thinking she wasn't ready for salvation beyond this earth, she fought, but to no avail. The hands were relentless, pushing past her flailing arms and her sharp clawing nails. They closed around her throat and choked off her air....

*Help me!* Melody cried silently, knowing that this time no one was going to come to her rescue. But the cry echoed in her mind over and over until her world went dark.

# Chapter One

"Is the special-effects generator giving you any more problems?" Logan Wright asked the technical director.

"Let me take a look." Fran ran through a series of wipes from camera to camera. "It's a go," she said.

"Good. Punch up camera one. Then do a slow dissolve between one and two."

She brought the cameras on-line as instructed while Logan kept his eyes on the vectorscope that was installed in the rack on the opposite wall. He tweaked the camera control units until the colors and levels on all five cameras were within technical specifications. As chief engineer of Wright Ministry Television, Logan had to make sure every program scheduled for broadcast met Federal Communications Commission standards.

He was scrutinizing a feed from a prerecorded videotape they would use in that evening's program when he heard his father enter studio control.

"Good afternoon," Osmond called cheerfully, though it was more like early evening.

"Hello, sir," Fran returned.

"Father."

Logan looked up from his work but only for a second. His father's checking over every aspect of his broadcast was nothing unusual. Still, Logan worried that he was doing too much. The doctor had been warning Osmond to take it easy ever since he had recovered from his heart attack and bypass surgery the year before.

"Who's the stranger in the studio?" Fran asked.

"Well, well," Osmond boomed. "Whoever she is, she's welcome. 'Be not forgetful to entertain strangers, for thereby some have entertained angels unaware.'"

"She looks like an angel, all right," Fran agreed, laughing.

Curious, Logan glanced at the shot the technical director had punched up on-line, then turned to give the monitor his full attention. A petite woman in a flowing peach-colored dress was standing on the set in front of an arched stained-glass window, its brilliant colors a striking contrast to her soft pastel beauty. The backlight rimming her waist-length golden blond hair gave her an ethereal glow that simply mesmerized him. Jim, the cameraman on one, zoomed in while she gazed around as if she were looking for someone. Her ivory skin was translucent, her face heart shaped, her mouth a perfect Cupid's bow. And she had the biggest blue eyes he had ever seen.

"The young lady must have shown up a day early for the choir auditions," Osmond mused. "Perhaps I should welcome her and straighten out the mistake myself. If her voice matches her celestial appearance..."

Logan couldn't stop staring at the monitor. According to the Bible, angels were messengers, appearing to mortals to portend future events. What might this angel's mission be?

Osmond clapped him on the back before leaving the control room. His father's touch brought Logan out of his trance. Still gazing at the woman, he spoke into the mike on his headset intercom. "Jim, do you think you can remember to cap your camera before we break for dinner? If I have to replace any tubes because of a burned-in image, the cost is going to come out of your pay."

"I'll cap the lens right now until rehearsal starts," the ever-forgetful Jim replied.

The monitor with the shot of the blonde went black, but not before Logan registered the fact that she looked not only angelic, but vaguely familiar. . . .

A PIECE OF DOVE-GRAY watermark bond curled around the black roller. After adjusting the paper carefully, gloved hands opened the book that lay next to the typewriter.

Osmond Wright would not get away with his sins without just retribution . . . and the afterlife would be far too long in coming. Now was the time! The self-righteous preacher would understand that when he received the note.

The concordance indexed several appropriate quotations, one of which made the point perfectly. A few minutes of clacking keys and it was done.

To Osmond Wright—

Hebrews 13.4. *Marriage is honorable in all, and the bed undefiled: but whoremongers and adulterers God will judge.*

You *will* be judged for your grievous sins. Repent now, before it's too late.

One who knows

There would be no signature. The paper slid out of the typewriter with barely a whisper. The televangelist would get the point, all right. Folding the sheet and slipping the note into a matching envelope, the author was already thinking about the next step.

BLISS GRIFFITH WANDERED around the bustling studio and tried to get her bearings.

"Excuse me." She smiled at a sandy-haired cameraman who was putting a cap on his lens. "Could you tell me where I can find Logan Wright?"

"Sure." He beamed back at her. "In the studio control room." He pointed to a wall with large, tinted windows through which she could make out a limited amount of movement. "You want me to tell him he has company?" the guy asked, indicating he could do so via his headset.

"No. He wouldn't know who I was."

The man shrugged and removed the headset before walking away. As she was about to head for the door adjoining the tinted windows, it opened and Bliss stopped. Out came Osmond Wright.

The silver-haired man was more impressive in person than on television. He was tall and well built, and even from a distance, Bliss could feel the effect of his penetrating dark brown eyes. At the moment, his face was lit by a smile, one that seemed to be aimed directly at her. Surprised, she steeled herself for an encounter with the minister rather than his son, then felt let down when he was detoured by one of the workers.

Unsure of whether or not to proceed with her original plan to confront Logan, Bliss found her attention drawn to a gravelly voice behind her.

"You've got to learn to assert yourself, sweetie," a brash but attractive redhead was saying from the nearest doorway. "Old Ossie won't respect you otherwise."

A young man with dark eyes and light red hair steadied the woman as if holding her up. "Mother, please, not now."

Bliss recognized him as Dean Mackey, Osmond's nephew by marriage. Not only did Dean occasionally appear on his uncle's show, but he had a weekly program of his own aimed at a younger audience. She could hardly believe that the loud, obviously tipsy woman was his mother, Joelle.

"Not now," the woman mimicked, tossing back her copper mane and throwing her free hand around. "That old fuddy-duddy hasn't had a new idea in years. You're always saying not now. When, then?"

"When the time is right, I—"

"At the rate you're going, baby, that's going to be never," his mother said, shrugging free of him. She narrowed her blue eyes and dug into a pocket, then pulled out a package of cigarettes and a lighter. "You're not afraid of Ossie, are you?"

"No. Do you have to smoke?"

"Worried about my health? Then what's stopping you from telling your uncle about your spa idea? 'Healthy bodies house healthy souls.' That's brilliant, Dean."

"It's not the right time to bring it up, however."

"Bull feathers!" She flipped the lighter and aimed the flame at the tip of her cigarette, then took a deep drag and sighed with pleasure. Smoke hung in front of her face as she said, "Health spas are big business. All we have is that small summer retreat around the natural springs. If people will pay a couple of thousand bucks a week to stay at some exclusive fat farm, they'll pay even more to stay at a place with healing waters."

Weaving forward as though she were going to approach Osmond on the subject herself, Joelle took another drag on the cigarette, releasing the smoke with seeming reluctance.

"Your uncle needs some youthful thinking to keep the ministry coffers full."

She stalked past Bliss, Dean following. He caught his mother's arm and whispered something as they neared the silver-haired televangelist. Osmond's brow furrowed as he stared at Joelle with a disapproving expression. Then he looked toward another section of the set and caught the attention of a lovely woman with auburn hair. He waved her over. Bliss recognized Lurlene, Osmond's wife, who hurried to her husband's side and took her sister in hand.

"Joelle, honey," she said, her Southern accent softening the effect of a firm will. "Why don't you and I make sure dinner is coming along? All right?"

"Anything you say, Lurlene, darlin'."

Bliss heard the mocking note in Joelle's words, yet the brash redhead allowed her sister to lead her out of the studio. Realizing she'd been rooted to the same spot for the past five minutes, she decided the time for stalling was up. As she was about to move, she realized Osmond was advancing on her, hand held out in greeting.

"How do you do? I'm the Reverend Osmond Wright." She took his hand. "I'm Bliss Griffith."

"Bliss, is it? Well, praise the Lord if you aren't exactly what we need to spruce up the choir." His face lit in a broad smile. "If your voice comes near to matching your heavenly appearance and name, my television ministry is blessed indeed."

Startled, she stared at the man. "I beg your pardon?"

"I'm afraid you've made a mistake about the audition date, though. Tryouts are tomorrow morning. Do you have a place in town?"

"Place?" she echoed, puzzled.

"Are you staying with a friend or relative?"

This was her cue to explain her mission. "No, I just arrived to find—"

"That won't be a problem," Osmond interrupted smoothly. "We have an apartment complex within the compound walls. Many of our single workers prefer to live here on the grounds when they join the ministry, at least temporarily. There are a couple of vacant apartments, and since you don't have kin in town, we would be happy to put you up for the evening. You can decide whether you want to rent from us or live elsewhere after the auditions, when you officially become one of our flock." He lowered his tone from hearty to conspiratorial. "I strongly suspect you're going to dazzle the choral director."

Bliss realized he didn't have the faintest idea who she was or why she was there. About to set him straight—that she was definitely not planning to audition—she hesitated. Becoming "one of the flock" might suit her purposes much better than remaining the outsider. She had a decent voice and had been in the church choir before her mother died. Why not?

"Thank you," Bliss said quickly before she could change her mind. "I hope I can live up to your expectations."

"I'm sure you will. Now if you can just be patient for a half hour or so until we block tonight's show for the technical crew, I'll find someone to take you over to the complex." He grasped her arm in a gentlemanly fashion and prompted her toward the doorway. "You can wait in studio control where you can get a better idea of what goes on behind the scenes."

"Great."

Bliss ignored her racing pulse, which was undoubtedly trying to warn her that she was doing something foolish—something that went against the grain of her practical nature. An obstinate voice inside her argued that a drastic situation called for desperate measures. And she had never been afraid to face a challenge.

Once inside the control room, Osmond introduced her to several people, including his nephew. "Bliss Griffith, the Reverend Dean Mackey. Bliss showed up at our door just when we needed her," he said with his natural enthusiasm. "She's auditioning for the choir tomorrow."

Dean gave her a speculative once-over and was obviously pleased with what he saw. "Bliss. Extraordinary how well your name suits you. And it's so...melodic."

Uncomfortable at the comment, she smiled stiffly and looked around the narrow control room. Her attention was drawn to the curly-haired man who was busy screwing a cover back on a piece of equipment. When she caught his sideways glance, Bliss was certain that he was more curious about her than he was letting on. Osmond then introduced them.

"Bliss, this is the black sheep of the family. My son, Logan."

Facing her directly, he gave her a long, appraising look that was somehow completely different than that of his cousin's. More personal, perhaps. Though a little self-conscious, she stared back, taking in the chiseled jaw, long nose and broad forehead dusted by dark curls. Finally he held out his hand. As she placed her own in his, she searched Logan's gray eyes for a clue as to the kind of person he was.

"Black sheep?"

His eyes glinted with wicked humor and his wide mouth pulled into an even bigger grin. "That's me. And I'm proud of it."

There was something about him—an appeal very much like his father's. She couldn't help but smile in return. "I guess every flock is entitled to one."

"And my son never does anything halfheartedly," Osmond said, his affection for his black sheep obvious. "Logan gives his all . . . or nothing."

Aware of the odd undercurrent that passed between the two men at the comment, Bliss diplomatically said, "I suspect he's rather like his father in that regard."

She wondered if she could trust Logan to help her. Would he give her all or nothing? Or would he betray her instead? Before she could make up her mind, the control-room door burst open and a tall, rangy man with graying light brown hair entered. His narrow face was drawn into a scowl.

"Logan, patch in the feed from CLN."

"What's going on, Gregory?" Osmond asked as Logan turned to the panel of complicated-looking equipment.

"Nothing good, that's for sure," Gregory stated. "But what more can we expect from a charlatan of Arden Heath's ilk?"

"Heath again?" Osmond muttered, his relaxed demeanor hardening.

A second later, the broadcast from Congregation of the Lord Network filled several monitors in the control room. Bliss focused on the image of Arden Heath, a Louisville televangelist noted for his fire-and-brimstone sermons. With his shaved head, black garb and stark, mist-filled set, he looked more like a representative for the other side than one chosen to do the Almighty's work.

"Again and again God speaks to us through the Bible to condemn adulterers!" Heath's voice reverberated and his eyes glistened with fervor. "'Abstain from fleshly lusts, which war against the soul.' To be saved, you must beat down your evil inclinations and rise above temptation. Throughout the centuries, God has sent us leaders to set good example. But we cannot always trust our eyes and our ears. I say to you, beware of the silver-haired, silver-tongued devil in our midst. He pretends to guide men to salvation while he—by his sinful example—leads them straight into the eternal flames of damnation!"

Shocked murmurs spread through the control room, making Bliss turn to stare at Osmond. No one had to tell her that Arden Heath was referring to him.

"Pull the plug on that idiot!" Osmond shouted. "I've heard enough."

"Father, take it easy," Logan said, his tone worried.

As the monitors went black, Bliss realized that Osmond was visibly shaken, his face suffused with color. He was tearing at the knot in his tie, loosening it, as if he were having trouble breathing.

"Uncle Osmond, are you all right?" Dean asked.

"No, I'm not all right! I won't be until that madman is banned from the airwaves."

Gregory clasped his shoulder. "What do you intend to do about Heath?"

"Nothing. He deserves no recognition from me." As Osmond spoke, his gaze alighted on Bliss and he grew flustered. "I seem to have forgotten my manners. We have a guest in our midst. Has anyone seen Hope?" He turned to his nephew. "Dean?"

The younger minister shook his head. "Not since lunch."

"Find your wife and tell her to set up this young lady in one of the empty apartments for the evening. I'm going back to the parsonage. We'll block the program for the cameras immediately before taping the show."

"Father, are you all right?" Logan asked. "I can come with you."

"There's only one thing I want you to do for me." Osmond's tone had suddenly turned unreasonable. "You know very well what that is." Then he stalked out of the control room.

"I'd better go after him," Gregory murmured, exiting as well.

Logan muttered something under his breath, which sounded like a curse to Bliss. When he realized she was staring in surprise, he initially seemed embarrassed before his expression subtly changed to one she couldn't read. Set off balance by the unexpected turn of events, she was both uncomfortable and unsure of her next move.

"Maybe I should head for town," she suggested as the crew left the control room. "There must be a motel in Wrightville. I can come back for the auditions in the morning."

"That won't be necessary," Dean told her. He pointed toward the window and the studio floor beyond to a young woman who was pretty in an unpretentious way. "There's my wife, Hope, now."

"You're sure I won't be putting her to a lot of trouble?"

"What does it matter? When Osmond Wright speaks," Logan said, his tone more than a bit sarcastic, "everyone is expected to listen."

He was still wearing that unreadable expression when Bliss followed Dean into the studio. She felt the oddest sense of relief once out of Logan's line of sight, and yet she couldn't stop thinking about him, which was only natural under the circumstances.

The circumstances—what had she gotten herself into?

She didn't have time to dwell on the dilemma once Dean introduced her to his wife and explained the situation. Suggesting she leave her car in the studio parking lot for the time being, Hope kept Bliss on her mental toes as they walked across the grounds to the nearby apartment complex.

"Where are you from?" Hope asked, tossing her windswept light brown hair back from her face.

"Indianapolis."

"A big-city woman."

"I've always appreciated country atmosphere," Bliss said truthfully, admiring the rolling, perfectly land-scaped grounds that surrounded the parsonage, offices and television studio in addition to the apartment build-ing.

"But Wrightville and the ministry itself are so limited. Are you sure you'll be happy here?"

Bliss couldn't fault the other woman for being curi-ous. Neither was she willing to tell her the truth, at least not yet. She purposely kept her answer vague. "I'm not sure about much right now."

"Oh. Working out some problems?"

"You could say that."

"Sorry. I didn't mean to pry."

Hope's sweet sincerity made Bliss feel a bit guilty. "That's okay."

"Most people who turn to God and to the ministry have personal reasons."

Bliss's motivation was very personal, indeed. She'd started out on this junket with a more straightforward approach than the one she now found herself embroiled in. Doing something so daring wasn't like her. A certified public accountant, she ran her life much as she did her work—neatly divided into careful ledgers.

"Do people often change their minds about staying?" Bliss asked, hoping to get some helpful information.

"All the time. Most people leave once their needs are fulfilled. We're used to the coming and going. Sometimes it's disappointing, though." Hope gave her a searching look when she added, "You get used to thinking of someone as a friend and one day that person just picks up and leaves without a word. She vanishes into thin air and there's nothing you can do about it."

"Oh." So much for playing detective. Instantly depressed, Bliss kept her questions to herself as Hope led the way into the building. The vacant first-floor apartment was more pleasant than she might have imagined. The place was light and airy, decorated simply but in good taste with pale gray carpeting and blue and gray furniture.

"Well, this is it," Hope said, hanging back near the door. "Furnished and supplied with everything you need except food. The store in town is open until nine. And there's both a coffee shop and a pretty nice restaurant if you don't feel like cooking."

"I'm not really hungry. I ate just before I arrived," Bliss said.

That she had lost her appetite was closer to the truth. Her stomach was shaky now that she was faced with going through a charade she'd had no intention of instigating in the first place.

"Well, I'm hungry, so I guess I'd better get over to the parsonage if I don't want to be late for dinner." Her brows rose in question over large hazel eyes. "I'll see you tomorrow?"

"I expect you will—if I measure up to your choral director's standards, that is. Thanks for making me feel welcome."

"My pleasure.

Bliss closed the door behind Hope, then wandered around the apartment. Could she really go through with this? She decided she would give herself until morning to change her mind. In the meantime, what was she going to do to keep her mind occupied? While she packed a suitcase, she hadn't included any reading material.

There was always television. She found the remote control and made herself comfortable on the couch. Turning on the set, she was greeted by the image of Osmond Wright.

"You must be born again here on earth if ever you want to see the Kingdom of Heaven. Does Jesus Christ live in you? In your soul?"

Bliss stared at the screen and tried to see the televangelist through neutral eyes. She had always respected the man whose sermons were positive and uplifting, but now she didn't know what to think.

"Change. Be willing to let God help you. Commit yourself to Jesus Christ as your Savior. He sees the good in each and every one of you."

His posture, the tilt of his silver head, his every gesture seemed planned. Bliss guessed they had become a natural part of his preaching rhythm. Osmond Wright had spent more than half of his sixty-some years in God's service, and hundreds of thousands of people had been drawn to his ministry. But not every member of his flock had actually moved to Wrightville the way Melody had, to work for the ministry as a panacea after an unwise marriage and a painful divorce.

"Only by developing a personal relationship with Him will you find the power of true love...true joy...and true peace in your own hearts."

Bliss pressed the mute button on the remote control.

If only *she* could find peace...and Melody.

Her sister had disappeared from this very apartment building the night before last and the police still hadn't a clue as to where she could be. They'd come to the conclusion that Melody had packed a bag and had left the ministry of her own free will. That there had been no signs of struggle in her apartment didn't mean a thing, Bliss thought, remembering the fear in her sister's voice. She'd told the detective in charge about the aborted telephone call, about the unexpected visitor. He hadn't been impressed.

After some hemming and hawing, he'd relayed the town gossip to her that had Melody involved with Osmond Wright on a personal basis. Why else would she have been promoted from a clerk with little responsibility to his assistant in the space of a few months? Perhaps she'd left after having been caught in a tryst with the preacher...and then, there were the rumored missing funds....

Bliss didn't want to believe either speculation. Her sister would never have an affair with a married man, no less a man of God. Besides, she knew Melody was in love with Logan, and after meeting the televangelist's son, she could certainly appreciate the attraction. Her sister was as honest as the day was long. No, she couldn't have done anything immoral or dishonest, nor would she have up and left.

Something terrible must have happened to her.

As if the thought could conjure her sister's image, Melody appeared on the television screen as part of the chorus. Bliss gasped, and her breath caught in her throat until it registered that CLN was running a prerecorded program. Still, that didn't keep her emotions at bay as the camera moved in on the young woman with golden brown hair curling around a face that glowed with happiness, framing wide brown eyes that sparkled with joy. Melody was so beautiful, so alive.

*Alive.*

She had to be. Bliss wouldn't believe the alternative.

She pointed the remote control at the television and turned off the power. Not used to feeling helpless, despite her small stature and delicate appearance—which always fooled people—she wasn't about to sit around and wait while the police played tiddlywinks. Taking care of her younger sister had become a habit since their mother died years before; she wasn't about to stop now, even if she had to resort to underhanded methods.

Bliss had left her business partner with all the work—for who knew how long—and had driven to southern Indiana to badger Logan for information about Melody. And if he proved to be of no help, she intended to harass Osmond Wright. But now she had an alternative method of playing detective.

She was willing to do whatever was necessary to find out what had happened to her sister! A chill shot through her as she realized that she might be making a mistake. She didn't know much about the real goings-on behind this ministry. Scandal *had* rocked the world of televangelism in the past couple of years.

Melody had told her that Osmond Wright was an honest man, and that his organization was beyond reproach. Although she would like to believe that, Bliss had natural doubts, which had grown with her sister's disappearance.

A polite rap at the door made her start. She popped up from the couch.

"Who is it?"

"Logan Wright."

The pulse in her throat jumped as she rushed toward the door. Halfway there, she paused, took a deep breath, pulled herself up to her full five-foot-three-inch stature and pasted a smile on her face. Only then did she go the last few yards and open the door.

"Hello," she said, further words faltering when she took a good look at her sister's boyfriend.

Leaning against her doorjamb in what she could only describe as a challenging stance, Logan had his arms crossed over his chest. His expression wasn't what she would call friendly, either. His brow was puckered and the eyes that had held such humor a short while ago seemed filled with accusation.

"Is it something I said?" she asked warily.

"More like something you didn't say." He paused before delivering the punch line. "Why haven't you told anyone you're Melody's sister?"

## Chapter Two

Caught in her own deception! Bliss realized she had no choice but to tell the truth and hope that he wouldn't blow the whistle on her. "Come in. We'll talk."

Logan strolled into the apartment as if he owned it. In a manner of speaking, he did, she thought, closing the door behind him, but his demeanor went beyond that of simple proprietorship. Bliss sensed an inner strength that she hadn't been aware of earlier...almost as if he had hidden part of himself in deference to his father.

He made himself comfortable in the larger of the two chairs in the living area, as if he wanted her to realize that he was in charge of this conversation.

Taking the offensive, he said, "You're the one who has the explaining to do."

Not one to let another best her—not even the man whose help she'd come to seek—Bliss leaned on the couch arm, keeping the superior position. She turned his statement back on him. "But you might have some of the answers I'm looking for."

"As in?"

"If you knew who I was, you can start by telling me why you didn't say something when your father introduced us."

"That's simple enough. I didn't figure it out immediately. You and Melody don't look anything alike. And your last names are different."

"Melody never went back to her maiden name after her divorce," Bliss explained, wondering why Logan wouldn't know that considering how close he and her sister were.

"I came to that conclusion when I finally placed your face. Melody once showed me an old snapshot of the two of you taken on the day you graduated from high school."

Touched, Bliss felt some of her pumped-up adrenaline drain out of her. She hadn't known her sister still carried the picture with her. "That was taken ten years ago," she said, keeping her voice steady with difficulty. She couldn't afford to let her emotions get the best of her, or she wouldn't accomplish what she came for.

Logan shrugged. "Some people never change. Melody told me you were the take-charge type. She said you looked after her and got her out of scrapes more than once."

"Someone had to."

"And that's why you're here now."

"I have to find out what happened to her."

"The police are trained for this kind of work. You're not."

"But she's *my* sister and I can do anything once I set my mind to it."

His eyebrows shot up. "You're awfully confident."

"I don't know any other way to be."

Bliss thought about all the responsibility that had been heaped on her at sixteen years old when her mother died and their father had been more burden than help. She'd done what was necessary then and now, twelve years later, she couldn't do less.

"According to the police, Melody—"

"Don't!" she exclaimed, moving away from the couch. "I've heard their version." She paced the floor in front of Logan. "If they're not willing to look further for the truth, I am."

"Through deception?"

She stopped in front of him. "I didn't come here intending to fool anyone. Your father thought I wanted to audition for the choir. I merely went along with his mistake. I thought maybe if I was 'one of the flock' I would be in a better position to learn something that would lead me to Melody."

"What makes you think she didn't leave of her own free will?"

Bliss stared at Logan. Considering his relationship with her sister, he didn't seem to know her very well. Unfortunately Melody was one of those women who thrived on dependency. If she'd gone anywhere on her own recognizance, it would have been to Bliss. She had always needed someone else's strength to get her through her crises.

"My sister called me because she was frightened. She said she found something she shouldn't have and that she'd been investigating. While I was trying to make sense of it all, someone broke into her apartment. Either that person forced her to leave or she ran away."

"The police told us about the telephone call. They went through her apartment thoroughly and found nothing out of the ordinary, no sign of a struggle. Some of her clothes and personal items were missing, however."

"And that, of course, is concrete proof that she left of her own free will, no doubt because the town gossip caught up to her!" Realizing she was so angry that she was shouting, Bliss told herself to calm down. She moved over to a window and looked out across the manicured grounds toward the parsonage. Taking a deep breath, she turned back to face Logan. "Do you, of all people, believe that garbage?"

"About Melody and my father having an affair?" He shook his head. "No. My father isn't the type to hit the front page of the scandal sheets."

Bliss sensed Logan's conviction wasn't as strong as he would have her believe.

"Any why are you concerned about my opinion?"

"Because of your relationship with Melody." Did he think she didn't know? Or was he trying to hide something? "As a matter of fact, I can't figure out why you haven't done something on your own about finding her."

"I wasn't exactly in the habit of tracking her movements. And maybe she doesn't want to be found."

"I thought you cared about Melody."

"I did. I still do."

Puzzled by her attitude, Logan stared at Bliss, wondering if she thought everyone else should look after her sister as she'd always done.

"If you care about my sister, how can you be so casual about her disappearance?" Bliss demanded, her voice filled with suspicion.

Suddenly seeing the light, Logan rose and moved to her side. "I never was as close to Melody as you seem to imagine," he told her. "I'm getting some strange vibes here. Look, I'm not sure what kind of a relationship you think your sister and I had, so I'll clarify. We dated until a month or so ago—*dated*," he emphasized, hoping that was concise enough for her. "We weren't meant for each other so we decided to be just friends."

"Dated? Just friends?" Eyes wide, Bliss gave Logan a look that would have cowered a lesser man. "I find your cavalier attitude disgusting and your story unbelievable. Melody was in love with you."

"Hold on. This is news to me."

"She told me love made her happier than she'd ever been," Bliss insisted.

"Maybe she was talking about some other guy."

"My sister doesn't keep a string of men. You're the only one she ever talked about."

"I wasn't trying to intimate anything negative. But be realistic. Melody was human, just as we are." Logan raised an inquiring eyebrow. "You are human, aren't you?"

Bliss stiffened and lifted her chin. "I'm not the one under discussion here."

"Perhaps you ought to be. Are you in love with anyone?"

"That's none of your business!"

"I see." Logan leaned closer. Had she been taller, they would have been nose to nose. "You're the only one who has the right to pry into other people's lives."

"I'm not a busybody. My sister disappeared, for heaven's sake! I'm worried about her."

Bliss turned away from him to face the window, but not quickly enough to hide the tears that were filling her big blue eyes. That was enough to make Logan back down. He'd been thinking that she was at least partly responsible for Melody's apparent helplessness because of her willingness to take on her sister's problems, but he couldn't hurt her with that truth. Wisely or otherwise, love prompted her actions. He appreciated her loyalty, if not her methods.

"I just want to find her," Bliss said softly. "I was hoping you could help me."

"Then why didn't you ask without all this subterfuge? I do care about Melody." He touched her shoulder in a comforting gesture and ended up feeling awkward. "She's a nice person. I wouldn't want to see anything happen to her. And I care even more about my father. I don't like the rumors people have been spreading about the two of them. Hopefully we can find your sister and clear my father's name at the same time."

Bliss turned back toward him—disbelief and hope seeming to war with each other in her expression. "Then you'll go along with my being here? You won't tell anyone who I am?"

"I'll keep your secret as long as you agree that we're in this together." His words prompted her smile, one that made him melt inside. "How do you suggest we begin?"

"In her apartment. Maybe the police overlooked something that would be significant to one of us."

"All right. We have a show to videotape tonight, but I can be back here around ten."

He was on his way to the door when she said, "Logan...thanks. I'm happy I don't have to do this alone. I feel a little out of my depths this time."

Something told him that they were both out of their depths, but at least they'd be in deep water together.

HIS MIND IN A WHIRL, Osmond Wright passed the platter of sliced turkey breast to Hope on his right. He'd gone to his study to catch up on some paperwork while waiting for dinner to be served. That had been a half hour before, and he was still stunned.

Another note had been waiting for him.

Another threat. But from whom?

The important question was whether or not the author really knew anything. It could be a bluff. Then again . . .

"Osmond?"

He realized his wife was speaking to him. "I'm sorry. What did you say?"

"I asked you if you wanted any mashed potatoes," Lurlene said, giving him a questioning look. "I made some special without any butter."

Osmond hated any reminder of his weakness. Why couldn't she have passed him the potatoes without bringing up the fact that she'd made them special? But he smiled and nodded and tried to pretend everything was normal, even though he knew it wasn't.

"Where's Logan?" Lurlene asked.

Osmond's brow furrowed when he realized his son wasn't at the dinner table. "I don't know. He should be here by now."

Unless, of course, Logan had taken his irritable comment to heart and was staying away from the parsonage on purpose. Osmond resented his son's refusing to live there, as if Logan's continued presence might weaken his resolve to thwart his father's wishes.

Having more important things to worry about than his controversy with his son, Osmond took a forkful of the special mashed potatoes, an ironic reminder of just how far he had fallen from the man he had once been.

BLISS FOLLOWED LOGAN to the top floor of the three-story complex several hours later. When he indicated the apartment that was her sister's, she stopped and stared at the door. Her stomach was shaky, no doubt because she'd chosen to skip dinner, but she hadn't wanted to leave the compound and chance missing Logan and the opportunity to do some investigating.

"Are you all right?" he asked, his expression concerned.

"I will be."

"Good."

He reached in front of her and turned the knob. The door swung inward.

Having lived in a big city all her life, Bliss was shocked by the easy access. "Why wasn't Melody's apartment locked?"

"Living in the compound is based on trust."

It suddenly occurred to Bliss that Hope hadn't given her keys to her apartment. "Oh."

"Go on in. I can assure you it's safe."

She flashed Logan a quick look. "As safe as it was for Melody? Without locks, anyone could have gotten into the place to surprise her."

"*Anyone* would have to check with the guards at the front gate to get on the grounds, just as you did. And there is a sliding bolt on the inside of the door," he said, showing it to her. "Besides, you don't even know foul play was involved. The police combed the apartment but couldn't find anything out of the ordinary. Look around, satisfy yourself. Nothing has been touched since your sister disappeared."

And, indeed, nothing in the living room indicated a struggle. The furnishings were similar to those in her apartment, the main difference being the beige-and-rose color scheme. The room was neat, all in place except a pair of shoes in front of the couch. Bliss felt her throat close at the intimate reminder of Melody's habit of kicking off her shoes.

She found the telephone on an end table and lifted the receiver. The dial tone assured her that the instrument was working just fine. Her forehead drew into a thoughtful frown as she set the receiver back in its cradle and remembered the frightening way the line had gone dead.

"There's another telephone in the bedroom," Logan told her. "Nothing wrong with that one, either."

Her eyes shifted to the open door. "You don't mind if I look around in there."

"That's why I brought you. I'm as anxious as you are to find some kind of reassurance—a rational explanation for Melody's disappearance."

Bliss nodded and led the way into the bedroom, which was also in order except for a blouse thrown over the single chair in the corner. She barely glanced at the few personal items on the dresser before opening the closet door. Empty hangers dangled from the middle of the rod as if Melody had recently removed clothes from them. Shoes were jumbled together on the floor. Above, purses sat one atop another in a hodgepodge manner, and on the higher of two shelves, an overnight bag leaned against a large suitcase.

Bliss knew a third medium-size suitcase was missing because she had given the set of luggage to her sister. Perhaps Melody *had* left of her own volition.

"Find something?" Logan asked.

He'd taken a seat on the edge of the bed as if it were a familiar habit. She wondered if he'd been telling the truth about his relationship with Melody.

"No, nothing," Bliss finally answered. She closed the closet door. "A missing bag, a few empty hangers. They don't tell me anything concrete."

And she was unwilling to believe that her sister would do a disappearing act without informing her, especially not after that call for help. Melody depended on her, and probably always would. There was nothing wrong with that. They were sisters, after all. Family.

Her gaze roamed the room again only to settle on the dresser. She scanned the contents on its surface more carefully this time as she crossed the expanse of rose-colored carpet. A hairbrush, comb and a tube of lipstick sat to one side of a table lamp. A box of tissues and a small framed photograph graced the opposite end.

She picked up the picture. Dean, Hope, a hunky blond man she hadn't yet met and Melody smiled at her from the simple gilt frame.

"That was taken a couple of months ago at Hope's birthday party."

Bliss hadn't realized that Logan had left his seat on the bed. Though he didn't touch her, he was so close she could feel his breath on her neck and it felt as if his heat was pressing against her. A delicious warmth spread through her limbs as their eyes made contact and a current passed between them. The dark curls dusting his forehead framed thoughtful gray eyes. She shifted her hip against the dresser to put more distance between them, then tore her gaze away and focused on the photograph.

"Who is this guy?" she asked, pointing to the blond good-looking stranger in the picture.

"That's our former television lighting director, Roger Cahnman."

"Former? He quit?"

"He was fired after being involved in a physical altercation with my father."

Bliss noted that Logan had worded his answer carefully. "Your father took this big guy on in a fight?"

She wasn't sure he would answer. His expression was closed, but she sensed Logan harbored a deep-seated anger about the episode.

Finally he said, "I haven't the faintest idea what caused the fight. I wasn't around. It seems that no one witnessed anything until Gregory found the two men rolling on the studio floor. Roger easily got the better of my father, of course. The bastard could have killed him." When Bliss looked at him questioningly, he added, "His heart. He had a triple bypass last year."

"Good Lord."

"He certainly is. He let my father get away with nothing more than a bruised jaw, a blackened eye and a couple of scraped knuckles."

An odd feeling chilled her as Bliss set the framed photograph back in place on the dresser. Had Melody been friends with a man who could be violent? A silly question. Most people were capable of violence given the right provocation. Figuring Logan wouldn't appreciate that observation—that Osmond might have been doing the provoking—she wasn't about to share the thought with him.

"Were Roger and Melody...good friends?"

"Not that I know of, but I didn't keep tabs on your sister." When she gave him a reproachful look, he protested, "I told you there was nothing serious between us. We haven't dated in months."

"So you said."

Bliss wished she knew what to believe. She couldn't reconcile Logan's assertions about his casual relationship with Melody and her declarations of finding happiness in love. Surely he would have sensed her feelings. Perhaps he merely hadn't wanted to recognize what he didn't share. When Bliss had tried to get to the heart of the situation earlier, he had sidetracked her with that business about whether or not she was human.

Was that his way of avoiding a confrontation or a guilty conscience? Bliss figured she wasn't going to find out easily so didn't push the issue. Instead she opened the top dresser drawer and began sorting through the tangled heap of lingerie that was quintessential Melody. While her sister kept her living space comparatively neat on the outside, her drawers had always been a big jumble.

"What do you hope to find in there?"

Logan leaned over and peered into the drawer. As far as Bliss was concerned, he was too close for comfort. She edged away from him as she continued her search.

"I'm not sure. I'm just following my instincts."

As if sensing her discomfort and amused by it, he smothered a laugh as he backed off. "Be sure to tell me when you find whatever it is."

"You'll be the first to know," she assured him as he reclaimed his seat on the bed.

Although she went through each dresser drawer carefully, Bliss found nothing that might prove a clue to her sister's disappearance. Unwilling to admit defeat, she roamed the room seeing nothing of importance.

"Give up?" Logan asked.

"No, of course I'll do no such thing." She stopped at the edge of the nightstand and stared at him steadily. "Not until I find her." She was unwilling to concede that she might be taking on the impossible.

"I could have guessed that. You seem dauntless. I meant are you through in here?"

Appeased, she didn't comment, but rather chose to check the telephone that rested inches from her hand. The extension was working exactly as he'd said. Rankled by the terrible feeling of helplessness that threatened to engulf her, she dropped the receiver into its cradle. With her confidence waning, she jerked open the nightstand drawer.

A rush of excitement shot through Bliss and her eyes widened at what she saw nestled therein.

"I found it!"

Logan was off the bed in a flash. "Found what?"

By the time she removed the book from the drawer, he was at her side, but she was too intent on her discovery to let the man's proximity disturb her. Her fingers trembled as they stroked the worn leather and her heartbeat seemed to trip over itself, making her chest squeeze tight. What had once been large gilt letters on the front cover of the book were barely legible now. She traced them with a fingertip, remembering how they'd faded over the years.

"This is Melody's Bible," Bliss whispered, her voice choked. Eyes stinging and filling with unshed tears, she raised them to Logan. "Don't you see? One of her suitcases is missing, and some of her clothes. If Melody had packed her own things, she would have taken her Bible. She never would have left this behind willingly."

"Come on, you're reaching."

Logan sounded impatient and pitying. Hot anger surged through her even as he continued.

"You haven't found proof of anything. I know Melody's faith was strong, but she could always buy another Bible no matter where she went."

"No! This one is irreplaceable."

Bliss was tempted to slap the sympathetic expression from his face. Instead she tightened her fingers around the book and pressed it tightly to her chest as if it could bring her closer to her sister. He put a comforting hand on her shoulder.

"Bliss—"

"Don't patronize me!" she cried, shrugging away from his touch and waving the Bible under his nose. "This is a family heirloom that was passed down from grand-mother to mother to daughter. Melody was twelve when our mother gave it to her...on the day she died. This was my sister's only legacy from our mother, and she consid-ered it her most precious possession. She never would have left it behind if she went of her own free will."

Logan's expression changed with her explanation. His brow furrowed as he stared at the evidence in her hands. "Unless she was in a hurry and forgot about it."

"Never!"

Hesitating for barely a heartbeat, Logan said, "All right. I believe you."

Bliss looked at him closely. Certain that he wasn't simply trying to placate her, she willed away the linger-ing threat of tears. Crying would get her nowhere.

"Thank you, Logan."

"What now?"

"We call the police. With this evidence, they'll have to make a real effort to solve this case."

"Don't be too sure about that."

"What?"

"You only have a Bible in your hand, not hard evi-dence. You're making assumptions based on intuition. You haven't found a weapon or a note or anything the police would consider concrete. I happen to believe in instincts. That comes with being a minister's son, I guess. Faith isn't based on hard evidence, either."

Bliss sank to the bed. "Well, I'll have to try my best to convince the police."

"And if they don't buy your explanation?"

"Then we'll have to figure out what happened without their help." She knew her voice was strained. The stress of the situation was multiplying. "I don't intend to give up in any case."

"If you contact the police, you might as well pack it in."

"What do you mean?"

"You'll have to reveal your identity, won't you?"

And her idea of becoming "one of the flock" would go right out the window. "You've got a point. We're on our own, then." Bliss hoped she didn't sound as if she were begging, when she was. Raising her chin a fraction, she looked up at Logan. "You are still willing to help me, aren't you?"

He nodded. "We have an equal stake in this. You want to find out what happened to your sister. I want to protect my father."

"Do you have any ideas about where to begin?"

"Not yet. The first step is to get you inside."

"The choir," Bliss said, remembering her audition in the morning. "I'm pretty sure I can do it. And then?"

Not even a hint of a smile crossed Logan's face. "And then we pray for a miracle."

# Chapter Three

Listening to several other women auditioning from her seat in the studio, Bliss figured she would need a minor miracle to impress the choir director. She was at odds after a restless night of worrying and wondering whether or not she'd too easily given her trust to Logan. How did she know he was on the up-and-up? He might want to protect his father—or himself. It gnawed at her that he hadn't wanted her to call the police.

"Goodness, what a voice," whispered a woman whose darkly bronzed features and luminous brown eyes were as striking as her own powerful voice. "If this lady doesn't make the choir, no one will."

"Don't worry," Bliss murmured, glancing at the closest monitor with a shot of the young brunette. "You sounded even better."

"Bless your heart. You know how to perk up a person's spirits." The friendly woman held out her hand, which Bliss immediately took. "I'm Erma Dixon."

"Bliss Griffith."

"You haven't auditioned yet."

"No, but I think I'm next. I just hope my stomach isn't as loud as my singing."

"Too nervous to eat this morning?"

Bliss nodded. Not only had she skipped breakfast, but she'd never had dinner the night before. She hadn't missed eating until a short while ago when her empty stomach began to protest. Then she'd been sorry she hadn't made a trip into Wrightville to buy groceries.

"Hang in there," Erma whispered. "It'll be over soon."

Those reassuring words were ringing in Bliss's ears when her name was called and she took her place near the piano on stage. Her nerves were taut, and she hadn't the faintest idea why she'd put herself in this position. She hadn't sung since she was a teenager and had been in her high-school and church choir. She only hoped she didn't make a fool of herself.

"What have you prepared for your audition?" asked Paul Nardini from his seat at the piano bench.

"Actually... I have nothing prepared," Bliss told the choral director. She pressed a hand to her stomach, which chose that moment to rumble. "I, uh, thought you would want us to sing something specific."

Nardini adjusted his glasses, which were balanced at the tip of his narrow nose. He studied her intently for a moment and Bliss thought she noted a glimmer of approval behind the thick lenses. Determined to make the best visual impression possible, she'd chosen a pale gold dress to set off her flowing hair and had carefully applied makeup that enhanced her delicate features.

For the first time in her life, she was counting on her looks to help her attain a goal, something she would normally consider distasteful. But for Melody's sake she would do anything, and could use all the help she could get. She'd been right to prepare so carefully. A camera picked up her image, which was duplicated on several monitors throughout the studio.

"Can you read music?" Nardini asked.

"Yes. At least I used to. It's been a while," she confessed.

The choral director slid to the middle of the piano bench. "Do the best you can." He pointed to the book on the music stand. "Try page 31. 'Take His Hand.'"

Bliss sighed with relief as she turned to the selection. The song was fairly simple, and one she'd heard before. She'd feared Nardini would suggest some upbeat number, which Erma had performed with such emotion, showing off her incredible vocal range.

As the piano introduction began, she spotted Osmond Wright watching from the back of the studio. A few yards from his father, Logan watched as well. Both men had been close to her sister. Did either know more than he was telling?

Ignoring them both for the moment, Bliss sang from the heart, out of love for her sister.

"WHAT DO YOU THINK?" Joelle Mackey asked her son as they watched Bliss's audition from the control room.

"She's interesting."

"I've heard better."

"Her voice isn't as powerful as some of the others, but it does have a haunting quality that's almost chilling. And her looks—Mother, they're perfect."

Registering the certainty of Dean's voice, Joelle tilted her head and studied the close-ups of the blonde on the bank of black-and-white monitors. Something she couldn't quite put her finger on nagged at her even as she silently agreed that Bliss Griffith probably was as close to perfection as they would find. Ambitious for her son as always, she considered the possibilities from every angle. Still, they didn't have to come to a decision right this moment. That could wait until the young woman's background checked out.

Joelle would do whatever was necessary to protect her investment.

Everyone considered her a harmless drunk, even her sister Lurlene who should know better. While Joelle often took comfort in alcohol, her little habit didn't dim her plans for the immediate future.

The urge for a cigarette hit her hard and she pulled the pack and lighter from her pocket. Oh, yes, she would find out more about Bliss if she were to be chosen as one of Osmond's "Singing Angels," his all-female choir. Everyone had secrets.

She thought of the ones she already knew.

A wry smile twisted her lips as she lit up the cigarette.

"Mother, you know Logan will have a fit if he catches you smoking in the control room with all his precious equipment."

Joelle pulled the smoke deep into her lungs and let it back out in a leisurely fashion. "Don't worry, baby, I can handle your cousin."

Just as she could handle his father.

Osmond had no idea what she was capable of doing. But he would, and soon. She was sick to death of being underestimated.

BLISS CHECKED HER WATCH. A quarter of an hour had passed since the auditions ended. Osmond was conferring with his choral director. She and Erma waited together for mutual support. When the televangelist approached them, he was smiling at Erma. Figuring the other woman had made the choir, Bliss wondered if Logan had betrayed her confidence, after all. Then Osmond shifted his gaze to include her.

"Congratulations! With your opposing looks and vocal styles, the two of you will make the most wonderful complements to my Singing Angels."

Bliss felt the breath catch in her throat. She'd done it!

Erma gave a shout, grabbed Osmond's hand and pumped it. "Thank you, Reverend Wright. I can't tell you how much this means to me."

"The final decision was Paul Nardini's, but I heartily approve both of his choices. By the way, everyone calls me Osmond."

"Osmond," Erma echoed with a big grin. "Well, neither of you will be sorry. I can't wait to tell my sister. I'm staying with her in Wrightville. I can leave now, can't I?"

"Of course. Just be on time for rehearsal this evening."

"I'll be back way before seven. Bye, Bliss. And congratulations."

"To you, too, Erma. See you tonight."

Bliss scanned the back of the studio for Logan who seemed to have disappeared. She'd thought he would stick around. They needed to discuss their next move—or at least to set up their next assignation. Maybe he was disappointed that she'd succeeded.

"Erma is certainly charged with enthusiasm," Osmond commented as the woman practically ran from the studio. "And what about you?"

"I'm as happy as she is." And far more relieved, though she couldn't admit that to the televangelist.

"I'm glad to hear it. I've been thinking that since you're new in town, you'll need a job. Singing in the chorus barely pays enough to feed a church mouse," Osmond admitted. "We desperately need help in the offices. The work load has increased and a couple of people whom we have not yet replaced left the ministry recently.''

Including her sister, Bliss thought, biting her tongue so she wouldn't say the words out loud. She had to stay on her toes, censure herself before she spoke or she would be found out. She wanted to be the one doing the finding.

''That sounds perfect,'' she said. ''I mean, I was thinking I would like to rent the apartment you let me use last night. Working here in the offices would be really convenient.'' And would give her an even greater chance to snoop around.

''It's settled, then. Praise the Lord if things aren't working out perfectly.''

''So they are.''

Bliss hid a pang of guilt behind a smile. Osmond Wright wouldn't be praising anyone if presented with the truth. And, for all she knew, he might be as honest and worthy a man as her sister believed. One way or another, she would find out.

''Can you start work today?''

''Sure.'' Her stomach growled. ''Sorry. I skipped breakfast.''

''Let's get you into the ministry offices. After I let Hope know you'll be working with her, you can get an early lunch in the cafeteria.'' He placed a friendly hand on her shoulder and led the way to another section of the same building. ''My nephew's wife is handling a mailing for donation requests. She'll be grateful for your help.''

When they arrived at the office, Hope appeared to be so harried that Bliss made her trip to the cafeteria a quick one. She ate, then bought a sandwich to bring back to the apartment for dinner. She doubted that she'd have time to go into town between work and choir practice.

She spent the next several hours stuffing envelopes. The boring routine was carried out in an isolated corner of the large room and she couldn't get acquainted with the other employees. How was she supposed to do any investigating?

Halfway through the afternoon, Hope asked her if she would be willing to cover the telephones in the finance office across the hall. Hope wanted to take a break with Susan, Gregory Townsend's secretary. Bliss agreed, hoping the task would prove more fruitful, but the phone rang constantly, keeping her busy. She was transferring a call when Townsend left his office and, frowning, stopped dead at her desk.

"What are you doing here?"

Put off by his sharpness, Bliss craned her head to look up at the tall, rangy man. "Susan's taking a break."

He grunted. "I have an appointment. Make sure no one goes into my office, including you. Is that clear?"

"Yes, sir," she muttered while picking up the ringing phone.

She was wondering why Townsend had been so adamant about her staying out of his office when Hope and Susan returned from their break. Having been put on hold by the caller, Bliss was able to pick up the friends' low-voiced conversation.

"I'm telling you, if Gregory knows anything for certain, he's not talking," Susan said. "I still say Melody Sawyer disappeared at a very convenient time. Now assuming the rumors about missing funds are true . . ."

"That's what Terence told his wife," Hope agreed. "If you can't trust an accountant about money, who can you trust?"

Susan laughed. "Maybe Melody didn't know a thing about the money. Maybe the rumors about her and Osmond *were* true."

"And maybe we'll never know why she left."

Her jaw tightening, Bliss determined she would find the truth and clear her sister's name if it was the last thing she ever did. The caller came back on the line, distracting her from the rest of the conversation. Then Susan took over her desk and Bliss returned to her own office with Hope. She couldn't help but treat the other woman coolly after listening to the gossip about Melody. If Hope noticed, she didn't let on.

Stuffing envelopes once more, Bliss worked until five, then went back to her temporary apartment depressed and wondering what to do next.

LOGAN KNOCKED AT BLISS'S DOOR at a quarter past six. He would have sought her out sooner, but a serious electronic failure had kept him at the studio. Her presence in the ministry worried him. If she made any noise to the media, she could be responsible for his father's ruin.

When the door opened he almost didn't recognize Bliss. He'd seen her confident, angry, determined, nervous . . . but never desperate.

"Logan!"

He stepped into the apartment and she slammed the door behind him.

"If I guessed you'd be this glad to see me, I might have postponed the emergency repair I just finished."

Bliss frowned at his joke, all traces of relief vanquished and replaced by pique.

"I was afraid you'd abandoned me to my own devices. They haven't been very effective today."

"What are you talking about? You made the choir, didn't you? And my father hired you to work in the offices. You're inside, exactly as we hoped."

"Now it's time for that miracle," Bliss said. "So start praying. I didn't learn a thing that'll help. All I heard was a rehash of those rumors about my sister and your father...and speculation about the missing money."

"Not bad for your first day playing detective."

He could almost feel her frustration when she said, "I figured I would get to talk to people, to ask questions."

"And raise a lot of suspicions while you were at it? Your directness might work for you in most situations, but this one calls for more delicate measures."

"You think I don't know—"

Logan interrupted before she could get her steam up. "Let's sit and give you a chance to calm down."

Despite her token resistance, he was able to steer her to the couch. Her flesh felt warm and inviting through the sleeve of her dress. She raised protective instincts in him that her younger sister never had. She sank into the cushions, and he sat a safe distance away.

"You're right," she admitted after taking a couple of deep breaths. "I haven't been able to think straight the past few hours. I've been leading with my emotions rather than my brain. Let's discuss everything we know or have heard."

"Starting with Melody," Logan insisted. "Her background. Her reasons for joining the ministry."

"She never told you any of that?" Her expression suspicious, Bliss asked, "What in heaven's name did you do on your so-called dates if you didn't talk?"

"Not what you're thinking, so relax, would you?" Irritated, Logan wondered if he was going to have to spell

it out for her. "Any discussion of our pasts was probably carefully edited."

"Why?" A dark golden brow rose with the question.
"What's lurking in *your* past so terrible that you couldn't
tell the truth?"

"I'm not on trial here."

"Neither is my sister."

"Sorry. Wrong choice of words." Sensing that he
would have to be open about himself if he wanted the
same kind of honesty from Bliss, he said, "As my father
told you, I'm the black sheep of the family. I go my own
way while he expects me to follow in his footsteps, not
only personally, but professionally. He is determined I'll
take over his ministry."

"And you don't want to?"

"No. While I believe in my father and his work, I don't
buy many of the stricter tenets of *any* religion. I can't see
that having an occasional drink or listening to hard rock
is wrong, for example. Actually I'm far too liberal, while
Dean is more orthodox. He's always wanted to make the
ministry his life, but Father is too stubborn to name him
his successor."

"Have you tried to make Osmond see reason?"

"I've spelled it out for him, but he does not acknowl-
edge what he chooses to ignore. That's why I went away
to school and didn't come back, except for visits. I
thought he would get the message. Then he had his heart
attack a little more than a year ago and put me in a
quandary."

"You wanted to be near him, no matter what you had
to endure. At least you had...*have* time. My mother died
so young, so quickly," she added, her tone sad.

Logan realized he'd been right. His honesty would prompt her to open up. He took advantage of the shift in conversation. "You said Melody was twelve. And you?"

"I was sixteen. After Mom died, I kind of took over. Melody was just a kid. She needed someone to talk to, to set an example, to give her good advice."

"To get her out of scrapes," Logan said.

"Yes, I've helped her out of a few bad spots. You make it sound as if there's something wrong with my coming to her rescue. Do you think I should have let the police close their files on her disappearance, maybe never find out what happened, never find *her*?"

"I didn't say that."

"I'm a smart woman with good instincts, and I recognize censure when I hear it."

The edge of her voice put Logan on guard. Bliss was getting defensive. He didn't want to get her back up, but he knew all about familial interference firsthand. He chose his words carefully.

"Melody left me with the impression that you often came to her aid before she had time to work things out for herself. I'm not judging your family dynamics, but I'd like to understand them better. What about your father? What part did he play in your lives?"

"Dad worked in the Gary steel mills, picketed during strikes, looked for work during layoffs, or drank to forget his problems and heartache," Bliss said in an emotionless voice that matched her suddenly closed expression. "He never got over my mother's death, never found comfort in religion as she had. He couldn't turn to his daughters."

"Sounds pretty unfair."

"He wasn't cruel. He didn't deprive us of the basics."

"Yes, he did. He deprived you both of what you needed most—him."

"We had each other."

Logan knew Melody had had Bliss, but was the reverse true? Not that he considered Melody a selfish person, but merely a weak one who had never developed to her full potential, so how could she give support to another? Perhaps that's why he'd never felt sparks develop.

Circumstances must have toughened Bliss, not that she seemed hard. She was so soft, so delicate that he wanted to take her in his arms and assure her everything would be all right. But he wouldn't lie . . . and his thoughts were taking the wrong track. It wouldn't do to get too close to this willful woman who, in her misguided righteousness over her sister, might have the desire to harm his father's ministry.

"Melody told me you brought her to Indianapolis."

Bliss nodded. "I got my business degree while living at home, then found the best job I could. I took her with me, while Dad moved in with his brother. Then Melody started college in Indianapolis. Midway through her third year, she quit to get married."

Wondering how much of her sister's life Bliss had expected to control, Logan said, "You didn't approve."

"She was too young. The marriage lasted for a little more than two years. When Joel abandoned her, Melody came back to live with me. The only thing that made her happy was her faith."

"So what was wrong with that?"

"Nothing. I have faith, too."

"It's just that you didn't approve of her turning to my father's ministry." Any more than she'd approved of Melody's marriage.

"I had my reservations," Bliss admitted, sounding defensive again. "Considering the scandals other televangelists have been embroiled in, can you blame me? If you think I try to run my sister's life, you're wrong. I didn't interfere when she became part of Osmond's television congregation, or when she moved to Wrightville. I hoped Melody would find peace and contentment. Instead she found trouble."

Logan sensed the magnitude of the distrust she was trying to control. He could hardly blame her; she didn't know his father the way he did. Her doubts made him wary, however. If she didn't get the answers she wanted, she could go to the media with all kinds of accusations. His father certainly didn't need that kind of publicity. The doctor had been trying to get him to semiretire. A scandal could kill him. Fear made Logan more determined than ever to find out the truth.

"Are you sure Melody didn't reveal anything of significance when she called you for help?" he asked.

Bliss shook her head. "She wasn't specific. As I told you last night, she said she found something she shouldn't have and then decided to investigate herself. Before she could clarify, the line went dead."

"That something seems to have disappeared with her."

"Maybe. And then again we might have been looking directly at whatever she found. How would we know?"

How, indeed, Logan thought. He voiced a building suspicion. "There's only one thing I can think of pursuing—the supposedly missing money."

"Even if Melody found this money, she wouldn't have taken it," Bliss asserted, her voice tight. "More than likely, you can look to someone in your own organization."

Now he was getting irritated. "That remains to be seen. I wasn't suggesting your sister was a thief. She may never have seen the money, but she might have found a clue that would lead to the guilty party—assuming the rumor is true in the first place. My father hasn't confided in me."

"Maybe he has reason not to."

Logan's temper surfaced. "If you expect me to keep an open mind about your sister, I suggest you do the same for my father!"

"I'm sorry. This is just so frustrating!" Bliss cried, flying off the couch. "Not being able to take a positive step makes me feel impotent. I hope they're *both* innocent of any wrongdoing. Okay? At this point, all we can do is speculate. If only we could find someone else Melody trusted with this secret, someone who lives here or in town. Who were her friends?"

"Melody was friendly with everyone."

"I know the kind of person she was. *Is*," Bliss quickly corrected, as if assuring herself her sister was still alive. "But did she have a confidant?"

"She and Hope spent some time together, but I don't know how close they were."

"Anyone else?"

"My father."

They both lapsed into a momentary silence. Rounding the couch, Bliss successfully hid whatever she was feeling. Logan shifted in his seat so he could keep an eye on her.

"Melody was so wrapped up in her work for the ministry," he said. "In addition to being my father's personal assistant, she helped Hope with special fundraisers. And, of course, she sang in the choir. She didn't have much spare—"

"The choir!" Bliss checked her watch. "Oh, good grief, it's a quarter to seven. I almost forgot about rehearsal. I have to leave now." She was already grabbing her purse from an end table. "We'll continue this discussion tomorrow."

Logan rose and beat her to the door. "I'll walk you to the studio."

"You don't have to." Her troubled-looking eyes met his. "I'll be all right."

He cupped her shoulder lightly. It was a touch of reassurance, nothing more, yet he had the urge to take her in his arms, despite his own caution. But she'd already stiffened, as if his concern were unwelcome.

"I thought I would check on that equipment I just fixed."

"Oh."

Logan thought she sounded relieved. How odd. And yet he felt a mutual wave of awareness sweep between them before they broke eye contact. Bliss led the way out of the apartment. Without touching, they took a shortcut directly across the rolling grounds.

"Where do we go with the investigation?" she asked.

"The money. Finding out whether or not those rumors are true. That's our best bet. I think I'll go over to the parsonage and visit with my father. I'll ask him about it directly. He has no reason to hold back that kind of information from me." At least Logan hoped not.

"In the meantime, I can talk to members of the choir and find out if Melody was close to any of them."

"I don't think that's such a good idea. You just can't be that up-front. You're not even supposed to know her. And if you talk to the wrong person, you might be the next to disappear."

Bliss started. Her expression was horrified, but she quickly recovered. Obviously that thought hadn't occurred to her before he'd voiced it. Both were silent as they walked past a large copse of trees that separated the compound's living quarters from the working area, then up a hill at the top of which sat the building that housed television studios and offices.

Leaving her inside, Logan checked on the equipment in master control. The on-duty engineer reported that the prerecorded videotape feeds were going out to the network as scheduled. Logan was free to head for the parsonage.

First he returned to the studio control room where he peered out at the rehearsal from the tinted windows. He only meant to check on Bliss, but he found himself watching her every move with fascination. Despite her delicate appearance, Bliss had an inner strength and sense of self-worth that were very attractive.

If he weren't careful, he'd find his perspective clouded. His loyalty was to his father, just as Bliss's was to her sister. He only hoped that finding the truth would leave Osmond's reputation unsullied and the man himself unscathed.

BLISS LEFT THE STUDIO shortly after nine. To get back to the apartment complex, she chose the same shortcut across the lawn that she and Logan had taken earlier. She could use a cup of tea, a hot shower and a long sleep. For a few hours, the rigorous rehearsal had taken her mind off her problems. But she had been left drained, her throat raw.

Descending the hill, she glanced east. A full moon shone from a bank of thick clouds, illuminating the massive parsonage that glowed softly against the blanket of night sky. Lights dotted each of the three floors. Was Logan still there talking to his father? Had he verified the rumors of missing funds? Tomorrow seemed a long wait to find out. She wanted to see him now.

The thought of their earlier encounter sent the blood rushing to her head. For a moment, she'd felt an incredible affinity with him. Yet she still wasn't sure she could trust Logan. For all she knew, the ministry was corrupt—and he was part of the core.

Bliss concentrated on the dew-covered grass path that could prove tricky for a woman in heels. The late May evening had grown cool and she realized that she should have brought a sweater. The fresh, crisp breeze was strong enough to make the long copse of trees vibrate with nature's music.

Hugging her arms around her, Bliss listened closely and breathed in the pleasant fragrance of spring with its light scent of roses. A twig snapped to her left and she caught a flash of movement from the corner of her eye. Telling herself it was only a rabbit or some other small animal, she continued on at the same pace.

She wasn't about to start imagining things.

The clouds chose that moment to curtain the full moon and the area was thrown into an inky blackness. Bliss stepped awkwardly. Her foot slid on the wet grass and her heel caught. She stumbled, barely preventing herself from falling. Gasping, she laughed giddily.

But that laughter died when a strong arm wrapped around her throat.

"What—"

An increase in pressure cut off further words. She fought blindly, pummeling the person with closed fists and kicking at his legs with her heels. She tried to prevent him from subduing her, but he easily got his free arm around her shoulders and trapped her arms to her sides.

Before Bliss knew what was happening, she was pinned to his chest and being dragged back toward the trees. She lost her footing and a shoe went flying, but her attacker didn't stop moving. He carried her along as easily as a child's doll. She continued to struggle and tried to loosen his grip so that she could free her arms, but he was too strong.

This couldn't be happening to her. No one had a reason to harm her. But this man was going to. She sensed it.

Terror made her struggle with more ferocity, but no gain.

Finally he stopped in the shelter of the trees and held her motionless. The arm on her throat loosened only to be replaced by equally strong fingers. His lips grazed her ear and she tried to dodge her head away from the moist warmth of his mouth.

He laughed and stroked her throat with hurtful fingers and whispered, ''Singing angels who poke their pretty noses where they don't belong find themselves in heaven before their time.''

Unable to move—frozen with fear—Bliss took a ragged, choked breath. Good God, he meant to kill her! But why?

No one knew who she was except Logan.

Panicked beyond reason, she felt her adrenaline surge. Somehow she had to free herself long enough to scream for help. As he released her chest to grip her throat with both hands, she struggled wildly, clawing at his wrists and face. He ducked and her hand made contact with a cap that flew off his head. The iron vise around her throat tightened. Pinpoints of light danced before her eyes and her chest felt as if it were about to burst.

Hearing a distant voice—were she and her sister about to be reunited?—Bliss accepted the void that waited to embrace her.

# Chapter Four

"Do you have to leave?" Lurlene asked her son. "Everyone seems to have deserted me tonight."

Logan rose from the uncomfortable but expensive piece of dainty furniture with spindly legs that his mother called a couch. "I scheduled an early meeting with my technical people."

"You wouldn't have to worry about the time if you moved back here where you belong."

"Did Father put you up to that?"

"Logan, don't you believe I miss you enough to be speaking for myself?"

He bent to kiss her smooth cheek. "Still can't take my teasing, can you?"

"Out of here, then," Lurlene said with a sniff. "Shoo. Go get your rest."

Before he went out the door, Logan threw his mother a kiss. He was disappointed that he hadn't gotten the information he'd come for, and he wondered what kind of emergency business meeting had kept his father away all evening. Strange that the rest of the family would have disappeared at the same time.

Starting to cut across the grounds to the employee parking lot where he'd left his car, Logan changed his

mind. Even though he didn't have anything new to share
with Bliss, he decided to stop by her place for a moment
and tell her so, or she might lie awake all night wondering. He veered off to the right in the direction of the
apartment complex. The moon peeked out from behind
the clouds, revealing some furtive movements in the stand
of trees ahead.

"Hey, what's going on there?" Logan shouted as he
jogged across the lawn. He squinted. Two people were
struggling...no...one seemed limp, unconscious. "Hey,
you! Identify yourself!"

The last of the clouds slipped away. The full moon
shone over the compound and cast a silvery-blue luster
over the man in dark clothing who sprinted away from
the scene. A woman collapsed to the ground, her long,
pale hair billowing out over her.

"Bliss!"

Dread washed through Logan. He ran quickly toward
her small crumpled form and hoped that he wasn't too
late.

AN URGENT VOICE called her name. Her lungs heaved,
automatically sucking in much-needed air. She gasped
and choked and coughed, but she was able to breathe.

More harsh coughs racked her chest. She managed to
open her eyes, pull herself up and prop her weight on one
hand. She was so confused...Logan seemed to be running at her. He closed the few yards between them and
dropped to the ground. Even as she instinctively jerked
away from him, her mind registered the fact that he was
almost as out of breath as she. His expression was ap-
prehensive. He'd been running, so he couldn't have been
the one who tried to kill her.

Who, then?

"It's all right, now. I'm here and he's gone." Logan gently smoothed away the curtain of long hair from her face.

"H-he tried to strangle me," she croaked, her throat protesting. She lifted a shaky hand to touch the injured tissue, then winced at the contact.

"Don't try to talk."

Logan pulled Bliss to her feet. Off balance with one foot in a high heel, she would have fallen again if he hadn't slipped his arms around her for support.

"My shoe." She looked around in bewilderment as if she could find it. Everything was a blur. Nothing seemed real, not even the attempt on her life.

"I'll get it later."

Before she knew what was happening, Logan placed one arm under her thighs and lifted her.

"Hold on."

She pushed at his chest. "You don't have to carry me." The words were forced and sounded odd to her own ears.

"You would try to get in the last word even after someone tried to strangle you. *Please* shut up," he ordered irritably, "or you'll tempt me to finish the job. I'm taking you to your apartment and I don't want to hear an argument."

Bliss didn't feel like arguing. She slipped her arms around his neck and rested her forehead against his cheek. Shock was setting in. She was beginning to feel numb and horribly frightened at the same time.

If Logan hadn't come along when he had . . .

A shudder racked her slender frame. He tightened his arms around her. She closed her eyes and relaxed—and pretended she was safe. He moved across the grounds quickly, as if she were weightless. Bliss could sense his urgency and wished he would slow down, and keep reality at bay a while longer. They arrived at the apartment complex all too soon. He didn't let her down, however, until they were inside where he set her on the couch.

No sooner had he released her than he moved toward the telephone. "I'm calling the police, then a doctor."

"No!" Bliss almost tumbled off the couch in her haste to stop him. "You can't do either."

"Are you crazy?"

He picked up the receiver, but she slammed her hand down on the hook to cut off his line.

"I won't let you ruin everything." Her words were a harsh whisper scraping against the inside of her throat. "You're the one who talked me out of calling the police when I found Melody's Bible."

"Look, the situation's different this time. This guy tried to kill you. The proof is already starting to show on your neck. You're lucky you got away with a few nasty bruises. For all we know that maniac could be attacking some other woman right now."

Bliss shook her head. "No. The attack wasn't random, and I wasn't exactly a stranger. That man meant to assault Melody's sister. He knows who I am, Logan."

She couldn't define the emotion that crossed his features, but she was certain he wasn't totally surprised by her announcement.

"How can you be so sure?" he asked evenly.

"Just before he tried to strangle me, he whispered something about singing angels who poke their noses where they don't belong finding themselves in heaven. Angels, plural. Melody was one of Osmond's Singing Angels. She found something she shouldn't have, then...disappeared." Bliss swallowed hard, unable to come to a more permanent conclusion. Part of her couldn't think of Melody as being anything but vibrant and alive. "Now I'm in the choir and taking up where she left off, so he had to get rid of me as well. Don't you see . . . somehow he made the connection."

"All right. That's an even better reason for calling the police. The Bible *and* the attack on you will convince them that Melody didn't leave on her own. Let them solve this case. It's their job," Logan insisted, waving the receiver in front of her face.

Though her impassioned speech had left her throat scalded, her nerves frazzled, a spurt of unreasonable anger gave her the strength to grab the thing from his hand and slam it down in its cradle. The shock on Logan's face was almost comical, but the last thing in the world she wanted to do was laugh.

"No police," she said firmly.

Logan stepped closer and loomed over her. "If you don't let the police handle this, you'll come home with me where you'll be safe."

Annoyed by his demanding tone and stance, which were undoubtedly meant to be intimidating, Bliss insisted, "I'll be safe right here. When you leave, I'll bolt the door. I won't be as careless as Melody."

"Any man with well-developed quads could kick that door in."

"And chance having a dozen witnesses running into the hall from other apartments? I don't think so."

"You're being unreasonable."

A renewed rush of irritation made her heartbeat quicken. "Don't talk to me as if I were a child, and don't tell me what to do!"

"I'm thinking of your protection."

"And I'm thinking about my cover!" she croaked with as much command as she could muster.

"What cover?" Logan's voice raised to a near shout. "It's blown."

"To this man, yes. Not necessarily to anyone else. I can still sing in the choir and work in the office without anyone watching what they say around me." She was having trouble keeping her strained voice at an even pitch and her emotions from giving way. "I can keep my ears and my eyes open. Maybe I can still find a clue that will lead us to my sister."

His gray eyes met hers steadily. "What if Melody is dead?"

"No. She can't be."

"But what if she is?"

Suddenly the whole situation was too much for her. Bliss burst into tears. She'd rarely cried since her childhood, and it humiliated her that she was doing so now— in front of a stranger! When Logan tried to take her in his arms, assumably to comfort her, she tore herself from his grasp and took an uneven step backward that almost made her trip. Totally frustrated, she kicked off the offending shoe.

He fumbled in a pocket and pulled out a clean handkerchief. Hesitating only a second, she accepted the linen square and used it to wipe her eyes and blow her nose. He took her arm, and with gentle pressure, forced her toward the couch.

"Come on. Sit down and I'll make you something warm to drink."

"I haven't been to the store yet."

"Let me check the kitchen anyway."

Logan left the room. Bliss took a shuddering, deep breath. While she tried to compose herself, she could hear him ransacking the kitchen cabinets, running water and setting a pot on the stove. He was gone for several minutes, and by the time he reentered the living room, she felt her self-control returning.

"The kitchen isn't totally barren. I found a bottle of concentrated lemon juice and mixed it with hot water and sugar. This brew might not taste too good, but it should help soothe your throat."

"Thanks."

She took the mug from him. Sipping the sweet-sour liquid, Bliss knew she should be grateful to the man. He'd offered to keep her secret and help her—even if for his own personal reasons—and now he'd saved her life. He was only trying to keep her out of harm's way. Resentment overshadowed her gratitude, however.

"Now can we discuss the situation rationally?" Logan asked, sitting on the chair closest to her.

"I don't want to discuss anything with you if you're going to insist that Melody's dead."

"Look, I'm not insisting on anything. I'm just trying to be realistic. Why would this guy try to kill you if your sister were alive?"

"Maybe he's afraid that I'll find whatever she did. What if he did try to kill Melody, but she got away and is hiding out somewhere? He might be afraid she'll contact me. For all we know, this guy might have been trying to frighten me off rather than kill me."

Logan's gaze shifted to her throat and Bliss fought the temptation to shield it with her hand. She wasn't eager to look into a mirror.

"All right. You've made a couple of good points," he conceded. "It's possible your sister is alive. I hope so. Let's go over what happened to you tonight. Tell me everything exactly as you remember it."

Bliss instructed herself to remain calm as she concentrated on that night's events. "Choir rehearsal had just ended and I decided to take the shortcut across the lawn. I remember thinking I should be careful because it was slippery with dew and I was in heels. And then I was just enjoying nature in general. The sound of tree leaves stirring in the breeze. The light scent of roses.''

"That must have been some breeze," Logan commented. "The only rosebushes on the property are in the garden behind the parsonage.''

"The wind was strong enough to make me wish I had a sweater. Anyway, I heard a twig snap and thought I saw some movement over by the trees. I thought it was an animal.''

"It was—the two-footed kind.''

Bliss shivered and took another sip of the lemon brew. "The area was so dark that I stumbled and almost fell. And then he grabbed me.''

"What did the man look like?''

She shook her head. "I never saw him. He came from behind and wrapped one arm around my throat, the other around my chest.'' Despite her resolve to stay calm, Bliss felt her pulse race as if it were happening all over again. "H-he dragged me back toward the trees. That's when I lost my shoe. I knew he meant me harm but I didn't know why until he spouted that stuff about singing angels.''

"What kind of voice did he have?''

"Deep, I think, but it was difficult to tell because he was whispering. I tried to fight him, but he was so strong. And then he started choking me...''

"Is there anything else you remember?''

"No, I don't think so. No.'' And yet something Bliss couldn't quite grasp—something, just out of reach— teased her.

"How big was he? How tall?''

She gave Logan a quelling glare. "How should I know? Nearly everyone seems tall to me." Because she was trying to figure out what was bothering her, she wasn't fully concentrating when she said, "My feet were off the ground and still he had to bend his head to whisper in my ear."

"Do you feel up to trying it with me?"

That got her full attention. "What do you mean?"

"I can hold you from behind the way he did. Maybe you can compare us and tell whether he was shorter or taller, broader or thinner, than I am."

"I—I suppose."

"Come on." Logan held her gaze steadily. "I promise I won't hurt you."

"I know you wouldn't. Now. I wasn't so sure when I was about to pass out." At Logan's censuring expression, she quickly defended herself. "Well, as far as I was concerned, you were the only one who knew my real identity."

Logan didn't respond to that. He merely stood and waited for her to do the same. Reluctantly Bliss set down her mug on the coffee table and rose. Even though they would be playacting, she wasn't looking forward to re-creating the ordeal she'd gone through.

When Logan put his arms around her, however, he did so gently. "Did he hold you like this?"

"Yes, his right arm was around my throat. But his left arm was a little higher, under my breasts."

He made the adjustment. "What do you think? Can you tell anything about his size?"

"I don't know. After I lost the shoe, he picked me up off my feet."

"I'm going to do the same. Tell me if I hurt you."

In lifting her, Logan pulled her snugly against his own body. Rather than reliving the shock and fear she'd felt earlier, she began to experience a different, more disturbing set of emotions. Aware of every inch of him that touched her, of the feel of his muscular arm under her small breasts, Bliss almost forgot their objective.

"Well?"

"Uh, he's about the same build, I think. Possibly a touch broader." But not any more muscled than Logan, whose hard chest and stomach pressed against her back.

"What about height?"

"Put your lips to my ear," Bliss said.

A rush of air tickled her lobe. His breath on her ear and his curly hair brushing the side of her face were making her body tingle.

"Well?" Logan murmured in the most distracting tone.

"I, uh, had the definite feeling he had to lean over some, so he must be a bit taller, too."

"I'm five ten, so that puts him around six feet, give or take an inch. Are you sure you weren't aware of anything else about him when you struggled? What about his clothes—do you remember anything unusual about the material?"

Bliss was becoming so distracted that she wondered if Logan had added something stronger than lemon juice to that drink. Her involuntary response to him was not only ridiculous but out of place. She forced herself to concentrate on the details of the attack.

"First I tried to pry his hands away, like this." Bliss demonstrated and, though Logan wasn't hurting her, she was equally unsuccessful in loosening his grip. Touching him so intimately only made her more aware of his natural magnetism. She gritted her teeth and fought the invisible bond that could hold her to him as surely as his arms. "Then he slipped one hand around my neck while he made the threat. And finally, he got both hands in position to choke me."

Logan lowered Bliss to her feet as he changed the position of his hands to duplicate those of the attacker. "And what did you do then?"

"I clawed at him." As she reached up, the memory that had eluded her only moments ago snapped into place and vanquished the last of her unseemly thoughts. "I knocked some kind of billed cap off his head!" Excited, she tore out of his arms to face him. "Logan, I don't think he would have stopped to get the cap before you ran him off."

"He didn't."

"How can you be so sure?"

"I saw him run. He was wearing dark clothes. But his head reflected the silvery-blue cast of the moonlight. He could have been balding ... or he could be fair haired."

The breath caught in her throat as the fire-and-brimstone sermon they'd all watched in the studio the day before came back to haunt her. Bliss stared at Logan. Though she was sure he had considered the possibility, she bit back the observation that immediately came to mind.

Arden Heath was bald, but to think the St. Louis televangelist might be her attacker made no sense at all. More plausible was Heath's warning and no doubt Logan's fear—that they had a silver-haired, silver-tongued devil in their midst.

WITH THE MOON at its zenith, Arden Heath sequestered himself in his study as he always did when crafting a new sermon. The room, which was paneled in carved mahogany and paved with a maroon-and-navy Turkish carpet, was dark and somber—the perfect setting to put him in the proper frame of mind. He took advantage of this glum enclosure, not only to set his mood, but to plan. Fire and brimstone were most convincing when well served, and he was preparing for the performance of his life. When the time came, he would be ready.

The telephone rang, interrupting his train of thought. He glanced at the array of buttons on the console to see which was lit. His private line. He set down his Bible and, before the instrument could ring a second time, picked up the receiver. The caller didn't wait for him to speak.

"I thought we had an agreement."

Heath grimaced and studied his heavy platinum ring that was inlaid with a fifteen carat black diamond. "We do. What's the problem?"

"You're acting too soon."

"I disagree."

"I'm telling you—"

"Don't dare give me orders."

"You'll ruin everything. The timing has to be perfect."

"Don't tell me my business!" the televangelist thundered. "I know all about sowing the seeds of doubt in the most efficacious manner...as should you after so many years. Trust me."

The caller laughed. "Trust a hypocrite?"

"You really have no choice, do you?" A sudden and uneasy silence met Heath's mocking question. "I see you agree. Is that all?"

"No. We have to meet to discuss new developments."

"Why can't you tell me now?"

"Someone might overhear."

"You know where to find me."

"I can't be gone that long without raising suspicion. This time, you'll have to come to me."

Even while annoyed that he would appear to be taking orders, the televangelist recognized the urgency of the request. "Where, then?"

The caller designated an acceptable place and time. Reluctantly agreeing, Heath lowered the receiver and stared at it thoughtfully. Nothing could go wrong. He was not about to get riled.

New developments weren't going to spoil his blueprint for ultimate success.

# Chapter Five

Bliss ignored the achy protests of her body when she dressed for work early Tuesday morning, but she couldn't disregard her reflection. A half-dozen dark smudges of varying intensity glared at her from the mirror. She rummaged in a pocket of her suitcase where she found a scarf with flowers the same shade of pink as her skirt. Wrapping the silken material around her throat, she executed a simple but stylish knot. The overall effect wasn't bad.

And more important, no one would ever know she had anything to hide.

Deciding to make herself some of Logan's lemon brew—hoping it would soothe her throat and strengthen her voice—she left the bedroom and got halfway to the kitchen when someone knocked at the door.

"Who's there?" She winced when the words came out a disgusting croak.

"Bliss? It's Hope."

She crossed the living room uneasily, not knowing what to expect, and unbolted and opened the door. Hope's hands were full, one with a bag, the other with a fresh bouquet of yellow lilies and white roses.

"I thought you could use a welcoming committee now that you're here to stay. These are for you, fresh from the garden." Hope handed her the flowers and indicated the bag. "I brought breakfast, too. I figured you hadn't had a chance to stock your cupboards and fridge yet. I hope you like cinnamon rolls with your coffee."

"Sounds wonderful." Feeling awkward after the way she'd reacted to Hope the previous afternoon in the office, Bliss stepped back. "Come on in."

Hope's brow crinkled as she walked in. "What happened to your voice? No offense, but you sound like a hoarse frog."

"I strained my vocal chords rehearsing last night. I'm not used to the discipline anymore. I'm sure it'll be fine in time for tomorrow's rehearsal, though."

"I've heard only praise for your talent."

"Nardini says I'll be able to join the Singing Angels on Saturday night's live broadcast."

"Great," Hope said, smiling. "So where do you want to eat? In here or in the kitchen?"

"Let's stay here. You can set that on the coffee table while I find something to put the flowers in. Do I need to bring out a couple of mugs?"

"I can get them." Hope set the bag down and followed Bliss into the kitchen. "Which cabinet?"

"Above the sink." Bliss poked through the lower cabinets looking for a suitable container to hold the flowers. "I think I'm going to have to be creative here." She pulled out a large cooking pot without a handle. "Maybe I can find something more elegant later."

She mustered a pleasant smile and told herself to take advantage of the situation. Susan had been the one who actually made the catty remarks about Melody. If the picture in her sister's apartment was any indication, Hope must have been at least a casual friend. Logan had also suggested the two women had spent some time together.

So...if she was clever, she would find a way to get Hope to confide in her.

The other woman remained silent only until Bliss had filled the pot with water. Then, as if she could read minds, she said, "Bliss, I was wondering about yesterday afternoon..."

Concentrating on her flower arrangement, Bliss forced herself to reply casually. "What about yesterday?"

"I got the idea you were avoiding me. Maybe I'm just being silly, but I sensed something was wrong."

She had noticed, then. "I was tired and everything seemed so overwhelming, especially the upcoming rehearsal. My nerves weren't in the best shape."

"Oh, well I'm glad I didn't say anything to offend you. I thought we might be friends."

Bliss noticed the anxious expression in Hope's eyes. "I could use a friend," she admitted, allowing the other woman to interpret that as a positive response. She wasn't sure she could trust anyone other than Logan.

"Terrific."

Lifting the pot of flowers, Bliss said, "I think I'll bring these into the living room. Your bouquet will make a nice centerpiece for our breakfast table. Are you the gardener in the family?"

Hope nodded. "Tending to the garden is the one duty I really like."

Bliss led the way to the other room. "Duty?"

"Being a minister's wife isn't a bed of roses," Hope joked behind her. "Dean doesn't care what I do as long as I'm involved with the ministry, but Osmond isn't so liberal. He'd fill my every waking hour if he could. I think he wants to make sure I'm too busy to get into trouble."

Though she didn't think it would be wise to comment, Bliss picked up on the other woman's stinging tone when she referred to her husband's uncle. Joelle hadn't seemed to think much of Osmond, either. She'd called him an old fuddy-duddy and said he hadn't had a new idea in years. Could there be trouble in paradise?

If so, Hope didn't seem anxious to elaborate. She removed a thermos from the bag and filled the mugs with coffee, then brought out the freshly baked cinnamon rolls that were already on small Styrofoam plates.

"This is such a treat," Bliss told her, removing the wrap from her roll. She took a bite and a sip of coffee. "Mmm. Delicious."

"Lurlene baked them."

"But you brought them."

"I had ulterior motives," Hope admitted. "I thought we could get to know each other a little better. There's never any time in the office. Now that you're getting settled in, I'm sure you must have some questions about the ministry... or problems you might want to discuss."

Bliss kept the mug planted between both hands and watched the other woman steadily. "As a matter of fact, I was bothered by something I overheard Susan tell you yesterday. There have been shake-ups in several televangelist ministries over the past few years, but I was hoping The Osmond Wright Ministry would be different—especially since I'm working at the parsonage."

"Goodness, you do sound upset."

"After thinking about it all night, I am a bit unsettled." Pretending reluctance to bring up an unpleasant topic, Bliss took a deep breath. The strong scent of roses assaulted her nose and reminded her of the attack. Her pulse quickened. She tore her gaze from the bouquet to look at Hope. "Susan mentioned missing funds and some woman who might have taken them."

"Melody Sawyer. She just packed a bag and left a few days ago without telling anyone where she was going. Any kind of clandestine behavior always stirs up rumors." Her hazel eyes candid, Hope set down her mug. "Personally I don't believe Melody is a thief."

"Why not? Was she a friend of yours?"

"Yes, although we weren't very close. I wish she would have told someone she was leaving, but for all anyone knows, she'll probably be back. I'm sure the fuss is for nothing."

"What makes you say that?"

"Well, she didn't have a reason to leave, at least none that anyone seems to know about," Hope stated. "And she left most of her things in her apartment. Maybe she decided to take off for the weekend with her, uh, friend and then stayed longer than she meant to."

Latching on to the *friend* reference, Bliss felt her pulse speed up. Maybe she would learn something useful from this conversation. She wanted to demand Hope tell her everything she knew about Melody and her acquaintances, but she managed to restrain herself. It wouldn't do to sound too eager about a woman she supposedly had never met. With difficulty, she forced herself to take another bite of her breakfast before going on.

"Did this Melody's boyfriend disappear as well?"

"Actually I'm not sure that she had one. She used to date Logan Wright. Osmond's son."

"I know who he is." Bliss wasn't sure how she did it, but she managed to sound disinterested. "We met in the studio when I arrived on Sunday."

"Anyway, several weeks ago, Melody told me Logan wanted to break up. I assume he kept to that decision, yet she was so happy that I figured she was seeing someone else and maintaining a low profile. Then again, she was Osmond's personal assistant. Maybe Melody was merely finding meaning and happiness in her work.''

*Or with Osmond.* Bliss didn't want to believe that, and not only because it would reflect badly on Melody. Despite the fact that her sister was her first concern, she didn't want Logan to be hurt if he were to learn something negative about his father. But she remembered her sister saying love made her happier than she'd ever been—and she'd never mentioned the breakup. Had she avoided the subject because it had been expedient, to cover up something her older sister wouldn't approve of? Could Osmond have seen to it that Melody disappeared before she become an embarrassment to his organization?

The stab of doubt she'd had about Osmond the night before came back to haunt her, spiced with a touch of guilt. The televangelist could have been her attacker—but she didn't want to believe that, either.

Figuring she'd be pushing her luck if she continued asking questions about her sister, Bliss changed the subject to one of interest to Dean and, therefore, to his wife. "I haven't had time to take a tour of the compound yet, but I hear there are natural springs on the property said to have healing waters."

"If you want to see the area, the road makes a complete circle of the grounds. The springs are at the north end," Hope told her. "You'll find a dozen cabins surrounding a couple of natural ponds. Water from the springs is piped into a bathhouse, which has both a swimming pool and Jacuzzi. But if you have a chronic ailment, I'd suggest you see a doctor rather than depending on a miracle."

Bliss was surprised by Hope's cynical tone. Odd that she wasn't more in sync with her husband. She was about to formulate a careful reply when an insistent knock signaled another guest.

"Who could that be?" she muttered, though she was sure she knew. "Excuse me for a moment."

She raced toward the door, but before she got halfway there, her caller knocked again, more demandingly this time, and incautiously announced his presence.

"It's Logan. Open up, Bliss. I have to talk to you, but I need to be at the studio in a few minutes."

Feeling the heat burning up her neck—she'd admitted only to having met the man once—Bliss snatched open the door. She gave him a furious glare and tilted her head to warn him of Hope's presence before he could say something else he shouldn't.

"Why, Logan, how nice to see you. Don't tell me you brought me breakfast, also," she said, noting the bag he was carrying. Undoubtedly it contained her shoe and she didn't know how she was going to explain that one to Hope. "Your family is really quite thoughtful." She stepped aside. "Come in, won't you?"

He glanced at Hope, then at her, his face expressing surprise before he carefully masked the reaction. "Hope. I didn't expect to see you here."

"Obviously not." She rose and dusted her spotless skirt. "I should be on my way. I need to stop by the parsonage before going to the office."

"I'll see you there shortly," Bliss promised as she walked the other woman to the door. "And thanks again for breakfast. It was fun."

"And educational," Hope said, giving Logan an assessing glance before she left.

Bliss closed the door behind the other woman and counted to ten before facing Logan. He was balanced against the back of the couch as if nothing were wrong.

"I don't believe you!" she said heatedly, crossing the room to him. "Demanding I open the door like that—you could have ruined everything!"

"How was I supposed to know you were entertaining Hope?" he asked with equal belligerence. "What was she doing here so early, anyway?"

"Playing welcome-wagon lady. She brought me breakfast. I thought it was very nice of her, actually. What are *you* doing here so early?"

"I brought you something also, but I doubt it's anything you'd want to eat."

Stopping a yard from him, she crossed her arms over her chest. "The shoe could have waited."

"Not just the shoe. I figured you'd be anxious to see this."

From the bag, he pulled a navy billed cap, a fancy *OWM* embroidered in deep red on its front.

Her pulse threaded unevenly. "Is that the cap I knocked off the attacker?"

"I assume so. I found it a few yards from your shoe," he said, raising the bag to indicate it was still in there before setting the small bundle on the floor next to the couch.

Bliss took the cap from him. Turning it in her hands and fingering the red letters brought back the taste of fear. "Osmond Wright Ministry?"

Logan nodded. "These were made for all the members of the softball team earlier this spring."

"Then it *was* someone from the ministry."

"It does look that way."

They both fell silent. All her doubts about the moral fiber of the ministry surfacing yet again, Bliss found accusations ready to roll off her tongue. Knowing they would only alienate Logan, she bit them back . . . for the moment.

"Who was on the softball team?" she asked and noted he seemed relieved.

"Melody, Dean, Hope. Vern, Jim and Fran, who work for me. Roger before he was fired. Myself. That's it. And before you ask, I still have my cap."

Bliss frowned at him. As she was about to say he was the only one she trusted in the place, she remembered she'd thought he was her attacker. Instead she asked, "Did your technical people know Melody very well?"

"I don't think so. Maybe Jim since he's on the floor during all rehearsals and tapings. Though I don't ever remember seeing them socializing except when we were playing ball."

"What about the others?"

"I already told you Hope spent some time with your sister."

"Dean?"

Logan shook his head. "Believe it or not, he is the shy one in the family. He doesn't make friends easily."

"A televangelist who's shy?"

"Blows your mind, doesn't it? I know how hard he fought to overcome his natural inclination to stay in the background. When we were kids, he used to follow me around, let me make all the decisions. I give him credit for pursuing the path he has and trying to make my father see him as a worthy man with his own ideas. At least occasionally. Maybe television allows Dean to free himself. I'm not so sure he would succeed in a normal ministry where he'd have to get to know his congregation on a more personal basis."

Amazed by the insight, Bliss sat on the nearest chair. "I didn't realize you two grew up together."

"Dean's father died when he was five." Logan hooked a leg over the arm of the couch and straddled it. "I remember because Joelle announced they were moving in with us at my sixth birthday party."

"Here?"

"No. Louisville. My father began his television ministry in Kentucky. He had a program once a week on a local station. This place was built several years later. Not all at once, of course. Organizing an empire takes time and energy."

Recognizing the odd note of discordance in his tone, Bliss couldn't help adding, "And lots of money."

"No one gets anything for free these days."

"Not even salvation?"

"My father's not cheating anyone," Logan stated tersely.

"I didn't say that he was. You're awfully sensitive about the subject, though. Are you sure you don't have your own doubts?"

"About my father's honesty? Never."

"And what about things other than money?"

"Are you trying to rile me on purpose? Or does this annoying approach come naturally to you?"

"I learned to question what I didn't know or understand early in life while you're used to people taking your word—or your father's—at face value."

"You don't trust my father, do you?"

"I don't know Osmond well enough to trust him." With equal candor, Bliss added, "But I would like to."

That knocked some of the wind out of Logan's sails. His gray eyes held hers, as if seeking the truth. His close scrutiny made Bliss want to squirm. She wouldn't give him the satisfaction of knowing he affected her, however, and so forced herself to remain motionless until he once more picked up the conversation.

"I assume that means you're still willing to give my father the benefit of the doubt."

"With some difficulty, but yes, I am."

"You certainly are honest if nothing else."

"I don't like playing games."

"Then why don't you just admit who you are?"

"I said I *don't like* playing games," Bliss stated. "I didn't say I couldn't or wouldn't if necessary. If I thought any other way would be of better use in helping me find my sister, I would take it. And what about you? Why are you really going along with my deception?"

"I told you before. I want to learn the truth just as much as you do. In addition to being concerned about Melody, I'm trying to protect my father. God help him if he has a relapse. He might not be so lucky a second time."

"Is that why you rejoined the ministry? You said you didn't want to be your father's successor, but that his heart attack put you in a quandary."

"You have a good memory, as well as an acerbic tongue." Logan pushed himself up from the couch and crossed over to the window that overlooked the grounds to the north. "I came back to appease him, because I loved him and wanted him to get well. I thought I could talk him into letting go of his desire about my being his successor. I also hoped he would let go of the ministry gradually, let Dean take up the slack."

"That's what Dean wants?"

"That's what my cousin lives for," Logan stated, turning from the window to face her. "He wants nothing more than to please my father and earn his whole-hearted approval. It's become an obsession with him. After Arnold Mackey died and he and Joelle moved in with us, Dean tried to replace his father with mine. Considering how young he was, it was only natural that he needed that kind of male bonding."

"How did you feel about it?"

"I thought it was great. I was secure in my parents' love and I'd always wanted a brother. My sister is six years younger than I. I love her, but we never had anything in common. Sarah lives in Bloomington, now. She wasn't cut out for this life, either. She married one of her professors and is happy being a faculty wife."

Personally Bliss thought Sarah and Logan had a lot in common . . . if he really was serious about not wanting to take over his father's ministry. They had both left Wrightville . . . only he had returned.

"So while you were growing up, you felt closer to Dean than you did to your own sister?"

"In some ways I still do. I thought Dean's hero worship for my father was great, especially as I grew older and Father made no bones about wanting me to follow in his footsteps. While I believe in the ministry—most of all believe in *him*—I never had the calling. I would have to change a lot of my life to be a minister. I don't pretend to set the best example, while Dean has worked hard to prove himself worthy. He deserves to take over when my father finally retires."

Bliss heard the troubled note in his words. "Does Dean resent you?"

"He never says so, but we aren't close the way we used to be." His expression sad, Logan shook his head. "My coming home to run the television studios changed things. Yes, I'm sure he resents me, and I can hardly blame him."

Bliss felt sorry for them. Once brothers in spirit, they'd been ripped apart by a legacy Logan had rejected and Dean wanted with all his heart. Even so, Osmond was holding out the ministry like some prize that would go to the best man.

"So what exactly is this big quandary for you?" she asked, pushing him further.

"I'm worried about Father. He needs to slow down. His doctor has been badgering him to semiretire ever since he had that heart attack." He shook his head. "That stubborn old man swears he'll work himself to death until I'm ready to give his life a try."

She sensed he was more torn about doing so than he cared to admit. He might not have the calling, but he obviously wanted the best for Osmond. Then again, who knew what secret desires burned deep in Logan's heart?

"It sounds like you're going to do it," she commented.

"I hope I won't have to. I've been thinking about giving my father's life-style a try, yes, but only as a last resort. At the same time, I'm promoting Dean's case. Unfortunately I seem to be getting nowhere fast. Father can be the most stubborn man I know."

Bliss felt as if she'd scored a hit. People change. Perhaps Logan had as well but was not yet willing to admit it. She considered Osmond's dilemma. Dean wanted the succession and he did have some of the family charisma, but personally she felt his cousin had been dealt the larger share. Logan could be a natural charmer when he so desired, and he had no trouble dealing with people on a one-to-one level. She was sure that Osmond recognized those positive qualities and she figured that was probably why the televangelist held out despite his son's protestations.

"Too bad you can't think of a way to change his mind," Bliss said.

"I'm beginning to think it's an impossible task. Father wants his son to be heir to his religious empire."

"Can't he just leave you the money?"

Logan seemed startled, then angry. Leaving the window, he moved toward her. He stopped at the couch where he set down both hands and leaned forward. "Money has nothing to do with this. I thought you were an intelligent and compassionate woman, but obviously I was wrong. You're determined to be like the rest of the public that sits back and criticizes what it doesn't know diddly-squat about."

He enunciated each word carefully, as though she needed his opinion of her spelled out. Instantly steamed because she'd been careful to spare his feelings, Bliss rose and gave him a healthy dose of the sarcasm that she'd been keeping to herself.

"Oh, no. Money isn't involved here. Your parents live in a house that looks more like a mansion than any parsonage I've ever seen. Osmond drives a Mercedes and wears expensive suits. But none of those things require money. Your father just prays for them and they appear, right?"

She could hear Logan's teeth grind before he asked, "And how should the head of a multimillion-dollar business live and dress—like a pauper?"

"Ah, so now you admit the ministry is a business. Well, I've heard this kind of proselytizing about money before."

"So help me, Bliss, if you start comparing my father to—"

"You'll what?"

At a standoff, they glared at each other, Bliss wondering what she'd ever found attractive about Logan Wright. He could be the most volatile, hardheaded, frustrating man she'd ever met. And, she thought with annoyance, those were his good qualities. That he could be kind, warm and even sympathetic when he chose were things she would rather forget...along with his having saved her life.

"I thought you needed to be at the studio," she stated. "You said you only had a few minutes to talk. You used up your time long ago."

Glancing at his watch, Logan swore. "Damn! The meeting. Everyone will be waiting for me."

They would both be late, but Bliss was not about to suggest they cross the grounds together, even if that would be the sensible thing to do.

"Don't let me keep you."

"I wouldn't think of it."

Already turning on his heel and heading for the door, he didn't bother to look back. Bliss only wished she were close enough to slam the thing behind him. Her sudden frustration was almost tangible, making her wonder why she was losing her cool. And why she was doing this to herself. Perhaps she should phone the police, tell them everything she knew. Surely they would have to act on the information she could now give them.

So why was she about to get her purse and rush to the office instead of calling out the infantry? Her foot made contact with something soft that flew along the carpet.

The baseball cap.

Picking it up, she stared at the red letters that reminded her someone in the ministry knew what had happened to Melody. That someone was worried enough to try to frighten her off if not actually kill her.

Why? Was she getting too close?

Or was that person convinced that something she intrinsically knew about her sister might help her find the solution? Maybe... just maybe there was. Who was acquainted with her sister's habits and idiosyncrasies better than she? Instinct told her that if she concentrated hard enough, the answer would come.

Her blood ran cold as another, morbid thought occurred to her. Melody might be alive now, but she didn't have to remain that way.

Taking the baseball cap into the bathroom, Bliss hid it in the linen closet behind a stack of towels, then found her purse. All the way to the office, she peered over her shoulder to make sure no one followed.

She tried to convince herself there were worse fates than being a sitting duck.

HOPE CHECKED THE CLOCK as the office door swung open. Bliss was ten minutes late. After the argument she'd had with Dean when she'd returned to the parsonage, Hope was edgy enough to let off some steam and inform the other woman that promptness was next to godliness.

But it wasn't Bliss who entered the office.

"Lurlene." Hope turned on the charm as the auburn-haired woman headed straight toward her. "What brings you into the office today?"

"Osmond suggested I drop by to see how things are going with this current mailing."

Lurlene, always the obedient little wife, checking up on her according to Osmond's instructions. Why couldn't the man just leave her alone? Hadn't he done enough to make her life miserable?

"Things will be going fine if Bliss Griffith ever gets here," Hope commented, her tone calm.

"Bliss. That's the new young woman with the arresting presence whom I've heard so much about."

"Yes, the celestial-looking blonde who's making all the male eyes in this place bug out."

Hope watched Lurlene for a reaction, but as usual, there was none. The older woman had perfected schooling her features and her speech, unlike her sister Joelle. A couple of drinks got that loose tongue wagging. Hope wondered what it would take to make Lurlene open up just once and say what she was really thinking. No one could possibly be as sweet and accepting as Osmond's wife appeared.

"Osmond thinks this Bliss will be the perfect addition to his Singing Angels," Lurlene said.

Osmond, again! Didn't Lurlene have a mind of her own? Didn't anyone who was close to him? It was his fault that Dean was so obsessed with the ministry that he didn't have enough time for his wife. Hope couldn't even have her own home—or her own family. But she would express none of her frustrations. By example, Lurlene had taught her to keep her innermost thoughts to herself.

Hope smiled when she tried a new tactic to get to the older woman. "Logan seems to have more personal plans in mind for our new recruit."

"Logan?"

That got a reaction. Hope could tell she had Lurlene's complete attention.

"Yes, I had no idea that they were involved with each other, but Logan showed up at her door this morning, demanding to be let in." Hope scrutinized the gracefully aging face that was already molding itself into passive acceptance. "I was there because I brought over some of your cinnamon rolls and a bouquet from the garden."

"That was kind of you," Lurlene said, in control once more. "And I'm sure the young woman must be appreciative considering how difficult it is to be a stranger in a new place."

How well Hope remembered. Though she and Dean had been married for three years, she still often felt like an outsider.

But not for much longer, she promised herself with renewed determination. She'd had the patience of Job— and where had it gotten her? But things were about to go her way for once. She was going to grab happiness and hang on to it with both hands, and no one, not even the pompous Reverend Osmond Wright, was going to stop her.

LOGAN FINALLY TRACKED DOWN his father in the parsonage study midway through the afternoon. He hadn't forgotten about the money issue he'd tried to pursue the night before, and his argument with Bliss had only riled him. No doubt she suspected his father had skimmed the treasury to augment his personal income. Well, he was about to get to the truth of the matter.

His father sat with his back to the door, staring out the window, undoubtedly contemplating his sermon for that night's telecast. As Logan entered the study, he realized the older man was so deep in thought that he wasn't aware of another presence.

"Knock, knock," he said loudly.

A startled-looking Osmond whipped his chair around. His face had a grayish cast and a drawn expression that immediately worried Logan.

"Father, are you feeling well?"

"I'm fine. You just surprised me."

He didn't quite swallow that. His father seemed to get hold of himself as he relaxed and sank back into the chair cushions, so Logan wouldn't refute the claim. He was here for a different purpose and meant to get some answers.

"Did Mother tell you I dropped by last night?"

"Yes, she said you had a nice, if short, visit. Your mother really misses you. Why can't you make her happy and move back here where you belong?"

"I'm the only one who can decide where I do belong. For the moment, I'm content at my cabin in the woods. It's comfortable . . . and peaceful."

"I put you under such stress, is that it?" Osmond demanded, his skin suddenly flushing with color.

"Please, don't start. I'm not going to let you pick a fight today."

Logan sat in a high-backed padded leather chair. A warm-hued teak desk separated him from Osmond. He'd always felt comfortable in his father's study.

"So, what's on your mind, Son?"

"I have something serious I want to discuss."

"Sounds like something I've been longing to hear, but I'm sure I'll be disappointed yet again."

Logan ignored his father's wistful tone. While he loved the older man with all his heart, he was wise to Osmond's deviousness when he wanted something. The dispirited act could be replaced by indignation and anger at the snap of his fingers.

"I want to discuss money."

"A raise? What in the world can you do with all the money you make now?" his father demanded. "You live like a pauper in that shack—"

"Not a raise, not my money."

Osmond didn't seem willing to be appeased. He shifted gears. "Your capital equipment request has already stretched the operating budget to its limits."

"It's not the equipment, either. I want to know about the missing funds."

The silence between them stretched just long enough to counter Osmond's reply. "I don't believe I know what you're talking about."

"I think you do. Are we in trouble?"

His father glanced at his watch. "We'll have to discuss this some other time."

"Now is as good a time as any."

Distracted, Osmond rose. "I have more pressing concerns to take care of."

"Like what?"

With his dark eyes glued to Logan's face, Osmond asked, "Since when have you been so interested in how I run this ministry?"

"Since now."

"Then you've changed your mind?"

"No."

Osmond shook his silver-haired head and circled the desk. "I have to leave right this minute or I'll be late for my appointment."

"What appointment?" Logan rose, but his father pushed by him easily. "With whom?" No response. "Where are you going?"

He stood there staring as his father walked out of the study. He watched his mother try to intervene to no avail.

Osmond kept going, leaving his wife calling after him, her stance unnatural and tone sounding bewildered.

Logan was not only bewildered—not to mention frustrated that he couldn't give Bliss an explanation—but he was more worried than ever.

"SURELY GOODNESS and mercy shall follow me all the days of my life, and I will dwell in the house of the Lord forever..."

Was Osmond Wright worthy of dwelling in His house? Bliss wondered before mentally shutting out the televised sermon. She put her ear to the door and listened intently. No sound came from the hall. Making as little noise as possible, she slipped the bolt back and opened the door. A quick glance around assured her she was alone.

Even so, her heart began to pound as she ventured forth from her apartment, pulling the door closed behind her. She'd waited until almost half past eight, when *An Hour With Osmond Wright* was fully in progress, broadcast live from the other side of the compound—and had seen Logan's entire family on camera. Now, with everyone involved in the telecast, she could safely search Melody's apartment again.

Fear stalking her, she slid toward the stairs close to the wall. She couldn't keep the memory of her attack the night before completely at bay. Senses alert, she was cognizant of every little sound, all of which came from behind closed doors.

Bliss practically ran up two flights of stairs, then controlled her breathing with difficulty. By the time she got into Melody's apartment, she had to lean against the door to steady herself and to suck air into her protesting lungs.

All day she'd been considering her theory of why she'd been attacked. Since she hadn't had enough time to do any in-depth investigating, she couldn't be getting too close to the guilty party. Or if she was, she certainly didn't know it. Perhaps Melody *had* left behind a clue. Bliss could have sworn her sister had intimated that she hadn't gotten rid of whatever she found, so maybe it was here someplace, waiting for her.

As her eyes adjusted to the darkened room, she forced herself to relax, but not so much as to forget to slide the bolt in place. She wouldn't mistakenly let down her guard. She would keep her head, analyze before acting, try to think as if she were her sister.

Melody's habits—she knew them well. What had she overlooked the first time she'd searched this apartment?

She turned on the light and gave the living area a cursory inspection, but as she had expected, the place was virtually free of her sister's influence. In all the years they'd lived together, Melody had usually holed up in her room—no doubt so she wouldn't have to hear a lecture about her messiness.

Bliss continued through the apartment, turned on the bedside light and wandered around the bedroom, which was almost too neat. The framed photograph seemed to jump out at her from the dresser. She picked it up and studied it more carefully than last time. Her eyes were drawn to Dean who was wearing a dark blue baseball cap—with red letters—that was tilted to the back of his head. But he wasn't the only man on the team. Bliss frowned and shifted her gaze to the other male in the picture.

Roger Cahnman.

With his blond good looks, he could probably charm any woman he chose to. Though she hadn't questioned

Logan about Roger and Melody that morning, Bliss remembered asking him about a possible relationship when
they'd searched the room together. He had denied keeping tabs on Melody, so she might have been seeing anyone. Could Roger have been the man her sister loved?
Then again, he'd been fired. Before or after Logan broke
up with Melody?

Realizing she was only distracting herself from her
purpose, Bliss set the photo back in place. She sat for a
moment and concentrated. Where to begin? What to
look for? She had to be more methodical than last time.

Melody's habits could be a clue. Disorganized closet.
Messy drawers. Ripped seams and hemlines often safety-
pinned instead of sewn. Notes scribbled to herself because she had a rotten memory. Things stuffed where
they didn't belong....

Maybe that was it. If there was anything to find, Melody wouldn't have hidden it in an obvious place. Bliss
began searching drawers more carefully this time, looking inside garment pockets and under paper drawer lin-
ers. Nothing. She turned to the closet, searched through
pockets in skirts and jackets, opened shoe boxes, even
checked the two remaining suitcases. Still nothing.

What then? Of all the places she would leave a clue,
where would it be?

The Bible!

Why hadn't she thought of it before. The Bible was her
sister's most precious possession, an everyday source of
comfort and inspiration.

Bliss almost dumped the nightstand drawer in her excitement. She pushed the end back in place even as she
grabbed the leather-bound book. Planning to go through
it page by page, she opened the cover. Halfway through,
she began to get discouraged. Her search was revealing

nothing other than some personal notes Melody had penciled in the margins. She touched a sample of her sister's handwriting as though it would bring them closer in spirit.

And then she felt it—a slight protrusion where there should be none.

Stomach churning with excitement, Bliss flipped to the New Testament. The Bible opened to Mark 7, and there, wedged in the spine, was a piece of folded dove-gray paper. Her hand trembled as she removed the paper and unfolded it to reveal a typed message:

To Osmond Wright—
Mark 7.12. *Therefore do unto others all things whatsoever ye would that men should do unto you: for this is the law and the prophets.*
You will be sorry you didn't look to your own sins, Osmond. This I promise.

One who knows

No signature. A threat. Do unto others...what did that mean?

Bliss was reading the missive a second time when the sound of a rattling doorknob shattered the silence.

# Chapter Six

Someone was trying to open the front door. Bliss froze, cursing her own stupidity. She should have realized the living-room light would be a beacon across the darkened grounds. She should have thought to use the flashlight that she'd left tucked uselessly in her car's glove compartment. But it was too late for regrets. Maybe if she sat very still and didn't make a sound, the person would go away.

A soft tapping at the door dispelled that notion. Whoever was out there was not about to give up so easily. Wondering what she was going to do now, she folded the note and slipped it back into the Bible.

"Bliss."

Her name uttered in a harsh male whisper made the hair on the back of her neck stand up. She looked around for a weapon with which to defend herself. The bedside lamp. Hand trembling, she flicked the switch and cut the light. As she was about to pull the plug, she was stopped by the familiar-sounding command issued in a louder tone.

"Bliss, open the door. I know you're in there. It's Logan."

Caught between anger and relief, she bounded off the bed and practically ran to the front door. How could he have frightened her so? She slid back the bolt and barely had the door open when he pushed his way in.

"What are you doing here?" she demanded to know, her reaction provoked not only by the man's unexpected presence but by the way his face was drawn into a frown that spelled out his disapproval. "I thought you had a broadcast to tend to."

"I did, but it's quarter past nine. I went to your place, but obviously the apartment was empty. I was trying to convince myself there was nothing to worry about, and so came up here on the chance that I would find you," he explained. "I'm glad you're all right."

His words calmed her a bit. "Sorry I jumped on you." She hated to show any weakness but felt it only fair to explain. "You frightened me."

His expression softened. "And I'm sorry for that. So what did you find?"

"Find?"

"You're hanging on to that thing like you never want to let it go."

Looking down to where his finger pointed, Bliss realized she had Melody's Bible pressed to her chest. "Oh, this. It's just my sister's Bible. I had second thoughts about leaving it up here, so I decided to get it. It'll be safer in my possession."

Unsure if Logan believed her, she loosened her grip on the book. For some reason, she didn't want to tell him about the note she'd found.

"I wouldn't want to take a chance with a family heirloom, either." A questioning smile turned up his lips. "So you didn't find any new evidence?"

"No."

Her too-quick answer earned her a penetrating look, but Logan didn't challenge her.

"Then why don't we go back down to your place before someone finds us here and starts asking questions."

"Good idea."

Happy that he wasn't going to ask more questions, Bliss followed Logan's lead. He threw the living area into darkness before opening the door and taking a quick look around. Then he hustled her through the hallway and down the stairs.

All the while, she puzzled over her reluctance to share her find with him. He had promised to protect her cover as long as they were working together, but she was deliberately excluding him. She rationalized that she hadn't had enough time to reason things out, to decide what exactly the threat against his father meant. *Do unto others*—what had Osmond done and to whom? Until she had some answers, she would keep the missive to herself.

Why break Logan's heart by making him suspect his father if she didn't need to? Some crank could have sent the note . . . but why had Melody disappeared after finding it?

"Coast is clear," he assured her after they reached her floor and he peered around the corner.

"I don't think we need to worry now, do you?"

"I won't stop worrying until we find the truth about what happened to your sister."

"Until we find Melody," she corrected, the secret note burning her through the Bible.

Logan put an arm around her shoulder as if to protect her as they walked down the hall.

She felt strongly about protecting him in return, and that confused Bliss. Earlier in the day, she would have told anyone who cared to listen that she disliked him intensely. Now she had to admit that would have been an outright lie based solely on her anger.

Though they seemed apt to rile each other at the drop of a hat, she liked Logan a lot. It wasn't just that she was attracted to him physically, although she'd silently admitted the fact the first time they'd met. There were characteristics about him that got to her on a deeper level. He could be vulnerable and giving, and that temperament in a man was a rare thing in her experience.

Although she'd never openly admitted it to anyone, her father's selfishness about keeping distant from her and Melody had colored her view of men. She'd seen them as being insular, self-protective—more as competitors in business than as potential lifelong partners. And the husband who'd abandoned her sister had only reinforced that negative opinion.

Bliss tucked those thoughts away as they entered her apartment. The urge to immediately hide Melody's Bible hit her strongly, but she didn't make a move. She didn't want to raise Logan's suspicions.

"Home safe," she said.

"I'm not so sure."

"What do you mean?"

"I still don't like your staying here. Anyone could have access to this apartment and be waiting for you when you come in alone."

Bliss dropped to the couch and took a deep, relaxing breath. She didn't want to think about someone following her or attacking her. She'd had enough of that for one day. The bruises on her throat and her still-rough voice were constant reminders of what she should fear.

"You could always walk me home from school."

"Don't joke about this." His expression serious, Logan stood over her, hands on hips.

"Sorry. I thought a little humor would break the tension." She smoothed her fingers over the Bible as if the contact with the worn leather could comfort her. "Looking over my shoulder is starting to get to me."

"It'll get worse."

Bliss met his worried gaze. "I can handle anything once I make up my mind."

"You're either incredibly brave or absurdly foolish. Maybe both."

"If you're trying to rile me again, don't bother." She rolled her head to the couch back and closed her eyes. "I'm too tired to argue."

She felt the cushion next to her sag, but she refused to look at Logan. Even knowing he was very close without seeing him was enough to affect her. She wanted to give in to an unfamiliar need, to ask him to put his arms around her and let her rest her head against his shoulder. But she wasn't that kind of woman.

"I'm trying to make you see sense, Bliss," Logan said. "I've had all day to think about what we're doing. Playing amateur detective might make a good movie plot, but it's too dangerous for real life."

"I suppose you're going to suggest I call the police again."

"I was going to suggest we talk to my father first."

That got her attention. "Osmond? You mean walk right up to him and say, 'By the way, Dad, whatever happened to Melody?'"

"I was thinking more in terms of telling him who you really are, and then asking him about the missing money. I tried to confront him this afternoon, but he avoided me." Logan's voice tightened when he added, "He must know something about the money, Bliss, though you must believe me when I tell you he isn't capable of harming another human being."

"I didn't suggest he was."

"But you were thinking it. Last night, when I told you about seeing your attacker—about the man having little or light hair—I could sense your doubts about him."

She couldn't deny the statement. "All right, you gave me reason to wonder."

"He couldn't have attacked you like that, Bliss. His heart couldn't take it."

"He got involved in a fight with Roger Cahnman."

"That was different."

"How?"

Logan shrugged. "I can't really say since Father won't talk about it, but I'm sure Roger left him no choice. Still, whatever his faults, my father isn't violent. He's a good man, a man of God."

"He's also human."

"That, too."

*Do unto others*—the phrase echoed in her mind, demanding an explanation.

Bliss thought to continue the argument, but Logan seemed almost desperate that she believe him. She couldn't go on to shake his faith in his father, but neither could she tell Osmond who she was. Not yet. Not until she was sure . . .

"Your father may or may not know the truth about the money, but that doesn't mean he would tell us a thing merely because I revealed my identity." Thinking the Bible and its contents would be safe hidden behind the stack of towels along with the baseball cap, she rose from the couch and headed for the bathroom. "I have a better idea, but I'm going to need your help."

"To do what?"

Bliss paused in the doorway. "To take a close look at the books. You get me into the financial offices and we can find out for ourselves whether or not the coffers have been raided."

GLOVED FINGERS PAGED through the Bible reverently. After all, The Good Book was inspiration for the missives that were making Osmond Wright's hands tremble and his soul shrivel. Such a clever piece of work.

How better to get to the televangelist than to use his own tool against him?

Finding the New Testament passage that best expressed the intended sentiment, the author set down the book and began to type.

To Osmond Wright—

Thessalonians 1.9. *And these will pay the penalty of eternal destruction away from the presence of the Lord and from the glory of his power.*

Your grievances against man and God will be measured. Then you will pay accordingly, both here on earth and in the afterlife.

One who knows

The author snickered as the gray watermark bond slipped out from the roller with a whoosh. Oh, to be a fly on the wall when Osmond opened this latest threat. He would finally begin to understand what was in store for him.

"ARE YOU SURE you have the correct key with you?" Bliss whispered when the first one Logan tried failed to open the door to the finance offices.

He stifled the impulse to start an argument with her, or better yet, threaten to strangle her if she didn't stop bugging him. He didn't think she would appreciate the black humor.

"Positive. There are only three masters for this building—one for the outside doors and general offices, a second for the television area and a third for the financial offices. That leaves this one." He inserted the key; the tumblers clicked. "There you are."

As he opened the door, Bliss switched on her flashlight so they could see what they were doing. He had agreed to proceed cautiously to protect her cover. Once in Gregory Townsend's inner office where the current financial records were kept, they could close the door, pull the blinds and turn on the room lights. Then she could go to work. While he was a whiz with electronic equipment, he didn't know the first thing about debits or credits. He'd be lucky if he could recognize a ledger if he saw one.

"Gregory's office is this way," Logan whispered, guiding Bliss ahead and to the right.

"I know where it is. I answered his phones while his secretary was on break yesterday."

They were halfway there when, thinking he heard a noise from the inner office, Logan stopped her.

"Wha—"

His hand clapped over her mouth, he placed his lips near her ear. "*Shh.* Turn off the flashlight."

For once Bliss didn't argue, but did as he told her. They stood in almost complete darkness, a faint glow coming from the hall through the frosted glass door. He listened intently. Sure enough, he heard a drawer slamming shut and some keys rattling as if the person were about to leave.

"Someone's in there and getting ready to come out," he said.

Thinking quickly about a place to hide, Logan remembered the small supply closet directly to their right. He put an arm around her waist and carefully felt his way in between pieces of office furniture. Though Bliss was breathing unevenly, as if she were on the verge of panic, she stuck to him like glue and didn't say a word. He wished she would follow his lead and his advice more often. She'd be a lot less trouble.

He found the closet just as the inner-office door opened. He barely got them both inside the tiny space and pulled the door shut soundlessly before the overhead lights went on in the main room, a line of brightness shining through the crack at the floor.

The person was moving closer. Surely they hadn't been heard.

Inside the narrow confines of the closet, they had hardly enough room to breathe. Shelves pressing against their backs and their sides forced them together. Boxes lining the floor constricted any movement. Sensing her building anxiety, Logan wrapped his arm around Bliss and turned her more fully to him so she wouldn't panic and lose her balance. She laid her hand on the front of his sweater and her forehead made contact with his cheek. Her uneven breath feathered his neck and her heartbeat quickened against his chest.

Despite himself and the impossible situation, desire flared. His hand on her back was mere inches from her small tempting breast, and her thigh was wedged tightly against both of his.

Footsteps whispering across the wooden floor reminded him of where he was, though the sound was slightly muffled by the closet door, making it impossible to tell if the person were male or female. Whoever it was paused directly outside their hiding place. Bliss stiffened in his arms. Though he, too, was worried that they might be found out, he didn't believe they were in any danger. He gave her a reassuring squeeze. And then the footsteps went on.

The glow of brightness at floor level was extinguished as the noise made by the hallway door closing told him the person had left.

Even so, Logan didn't let go of Bliss.

Since he'd first seen her in front of the stained-glass backdrop, he'd been fighting his attraction to the woman. She was not only impossible but questioned everything he'd been raised to believe in. Now desire superseded their inevitable disagreements, memories of which faded in the wake of an all-too-consuming physical need.

He could think of more provocative and satisfying ways to spend the evening than searching through files and studying ledgers.

"You can let go of me now," she said softly.

Her voice was unsteady. From the scare? Or was she as caught up as he by mutual attraction? She was making no move to extricate herself. He lowered his head, ran his cheek down the side of her face.

"What if I don't want to."

Bliss was very still, but her breath came faster than it had when the footsteps approached their hiding place. And her heart beat strongly against his chest.

"We've got things to do," she protested.

"Urgent things. Starting with this."

Even in the dark, he found her easily. She trembled at the contact, but her mouth parted, giving him her consent. As he caressed her lips, ran his tongue across her teeth until she met him stroke for stroke, Logan felt his desire for her grow. He cupped her breast through her cotton sweater and felt the nipple harden at his touch. The arousal in his body clouded his senses until he couldn't think straight.

But obviously Bliss could. She pulled her mouth away and pressed at his chest.

"This isn't why we're here."

He groaned. "At the moment, you're all I can think of."

"Well, think again." She wiggled out of his embrace, though the closet wasn't big enough to put much room between them. "My sister. Your father. Rumors about them having an affair. The missing money."

"I don't know how you do it."

"What?"

"You always manage to work the subject around to your advantage at the wrong time."

"There may never be a right time for us, and I think you know it as well as I do."

With that stiffly issued observation, she switched on her flashlight and led the way out of the closet. Disgruntled, Logan followed. Once inside the inner office, he adjusted the blinds and sat in the high-backed chair behind the desk. Trying to make himself comfortable, he shifted around in the seat and said, "You can turn on the light."

Bliss did so but looked everywhere in the room except at him. She couldn't meet his eyes. Logan smiled. She might talk a good game, but she'd been every bit as affected by that kiss as he.

"Does Gregory Townsend usually work so late?" she asked, setting her flashlight on the desk before perusing a row of leather-bound books on a shelf.

"Once in a while, but I don't make it my business to follow his habits."

Making her selection, she placed the book on the side of the desk opposite him, then pulled up a chair and sat on the edge. When she opened the leather cover and turned to the first page with entries, Logan realized the book was the current ledger. She pulled a small calculator from her skirt pocket. Her eyes were glued to the page, though he didn't think the numbers were registering with her yet.

"I asked about Townsend because I wasn't sure the person in here was a man," she said. "If so, he couldn't have been very heavy. The footsteps were too soft. While your financial manager is on the thin side, he's tall and has broad shoulders, and he'd have fairly heavy footsteps if he were walking normally. Then again, it could have been a man purposely sneaking around."

"Pretty observant considering how on edge you were." Logan figured he would get an argument if he dared use the word frightened. "I thought I couldn't tell if it was a man or woman because the door muffled the sound."

"Maybe," she said.

"Well, it doesn't really matter what sex the person was, does it? Whoever was in this office working late wasn't a threat to you—not physically."

"Don't be so sure." Bliss finally met his eyes across the desk. "I don't trust anyone around here but you, and sometimes I wonder if that isn't a mistake."

"Thank you very much. Next time I see someone strangling you, I won't interfere."

Logan was instantly sorry he allowed the heated words out of his mouth. Bliss's hand went to her throat, and she turned pale; her eyes looked too large for her fragile face.

"I know you saved me from that attacker, and I'm thankful for that. I also know you have loyalties as strong as my own. I can't blame you, but I have to be realistic. We don't have the same priorities."

He didn't like the sound of that. She really could make him edgy when she chose. "I want to find the truth and get it out into the open as much as you do."

"I wonder. You never know what we'll find. Maybe Osmond is innocent of any wrongdoing, but your father isn't the only member of your family you would be eager to protect." Bliss shook her head. "I'm not sure what you would or would not be willing to cover up."

He neither liked the implication that some other family member might be involved in Melody's disappearance, nor the not-so-subtle insinuation that he would volunteer to be an accessory to a possible crime. She was reaching and he wasn't about to stand still and let her voice such allegations without reprimand.

"Don't start making veiled slurs when you have nothing to base them on," he told her. "And get this straight, whatever you might think about my background in this ministry, my parents raised me to have ethics. That would have been impossible for me to learn if they hadn't set a good example. You have a lot of nerve casting doubt on me now. I could have blown the whistle on you from the first. Remember that."

Not deigning to continue the argument, Bliss turned her full attention to the ledger while Logan stewed.

He found he couldn't sit still. Other than fetching myriad folders filled with materials she needed from the files, he alternated pacing around the desk, inspecting the financial director's extensive assortment of equipment—including an old typewriter next to his computer—and making long forays into the darkened outer room so he wouldn't go stir-crazy. On the pretext of keeping watch, he peered out into the hall to make sure no one was around. In reality, he thought it a fool's errand.

So why was he being so protective? Why did he let that slip of a woman get to him on a gut level? He ought to reveal her cover and let the police find Melody. He wouldn't back out now, however, because he respected Bliss and admired what she was trying to do.

He might not like her suspicions and insinuations concerning the ministry and his family members, but he could understand and forgive them.

She was from the outside, influenced by the media, and didn't know his father or his accomplishments. The Osmond Wright Ministry made a difference to people, not only spiritually but physically as well. It supported a shelter for battered women and children in Indianapolis, a state-wide educational fund for promising teenagers from low-income families and several health clinics in a three-state area for those who couldn't afford insurance or the cost of medical care. Bliss probably had never investigated those things.

When he reentered the inner office yet again to see if there was something she needed, he found her making notes, her expression troubled. A file lay open next to the ledger and papers were spread chaotically in front of her.

"Find something?" he asked.

She nodded. "Are these all the promissory contribution pledges since the beginning of the year?"

"All but the current file for this month. Why? What's going on?"

"I found several credit entries that don't match the pledges. See this one? A pledge of fifteen thousand dollars by Mrs. Ava Turner. Yet the ledger entry says she contributed only five thousand and there's nothing on the statement to indicate she altered her pledge. And here's another for nine thousand from Sam Wolenski. That was entered as nine hundred. And there are others as cleverly modified.''

"How much money?"

"Almost fifty thousand dollars." She looked at him intently. "Don't you see what this means?"

"Yes. That the ministry is being systematically ripped off."

"But not by my sister," Bliss said triumphantly. "Melody might have had access to cash people sent in. Maybe she made deposits and being Osmond's assistant she could have received cash back. But she's not a book-keeper, so it wouldn't make sense for her to have had access to all of this. And while several different people worked on the ledger, all the falsified entries were done by the same person."

Logan looked over her shoulder at the open book. "You may know Melody's handwriting, but these entries are printed. That's not much to go on."

"Maybe not, but even when they print, left-handed people give their letters a definite slant. The falsified entries were made by a right-handed person."

"And Melody is left-handed." Logan remembered noting the fact the first time they'd had dinner together. "So who the hell could be responsible?"

"Do you trust your financial director?"

"Gregory? Of course. He's my father's best friend and has been with the ministry practically from the beginning."

"You said you thought your father knew something about the missing funds, that he avoided you when you tried to talk about them. Maybe because he knows it's his old friend.''

"No, the thief must be someone else. Gregory is completely loyal." Circling the desk, Logan thought about it. His father's friend had never given any indication otherwise. "No, definitely not Gregory. But no matter who is responsible, how would these missing funds tie in with Melody's disappearance?"

"I don't know."

Logan sat down in the chair opposite Bliss and rolled it back until it caught on something. "Maybe we've come to a dead end."

"I'm not giving up."

"I didn't say you should." He reached down and tore free a piece of gray paper where it had caught in one of the wheels of his chair. "I was merely suggesting that we're looking in the wrong direction."

He was about to chuck the paper in the wastebasket when Bliss said, "What's that?"

Logan held it up so she could see. "Just a piece of blank paper." He was puzzled by her odd expression. "Something wrong?"

"No, nothing." She quickly averted her eyes and gathered the contribution pledges, then straightened the pile before splitting and replacing them in the correct files. "I was worried I dropped one of these. It wouldn't do to let the guilty party know we're on his trail."

Somehow he thought there was more to her discomfort than she was letting on, but he didn't press the issue. Maybe he was getting as paranoid as she. It was half past two and they both needed some sleep. It would be heaven to do so wrapped in each other's arms; Logan told himself he was crazy. If ever there was a woman all wrong for him, her name was Bliss Griffith.

THREE IN THE MORNING and Bliss knew she wouldn't sleep if she went directly to bed. Nerves had nothing to do with her restlessness. Logan had walked her home and checked her apartment thoroughly before leaving, so there was nothing to be afraid of.

But there was the memory of his kiss in the closet that still plagued her.

And there was the piece of gray paper.

Fetching Melody's Bible, she unfolded the note. The gray bond seemed to be from the same stock as the piece Logan had found on the floor. Was the paper commonly used for ministry correspondence? Or had the person who'd issued the "Do unto others" threat typed another in Gregory's office? A chill shot through her as she realized the villain might have been in the room while she and Logan hid in the closet.

But who? A woman, as she had first guessed? Or a man who could be both light on his feet, yet strong enough to pick her up off hers as if she weighed nothing?

Not wanting to recount her attack, Bliss stuffed the Bible back behind the towels and wandered into the living room. Exhausted but not sleepy, she turned on the television, which was still tuned to Congregation of the Lord Network.

She sank to the couch and kicked off her heels as the image of Arden Heath appeared, swathed in black garb and man-made fog. Again she thought the Louisville televangelist presented an ominous figure, one that would frighten his followers into seeking salvation rather than leading them gently by the hand as Osmond did.

"Before I close, I want to read to you from The New Testament, The General Epistle of Jude, six and seven."

The camera pulled out as Heath stepped over to a giant open Bible. He set his hands on either side of the pedestal and looked straight into the camera.

" 'And the angels that kept not their first estate, but left their own habitation, He hath reserved in everlasting chains under darkness unto the judgment of the great day.' " He dipped his eyes to the Bible and the light shimmered off his bald pate. " 'Even as Sodom and Gomorrah and the cities about them in like manner, giving themselves over to fornication, and going after strange flesh, are set forth for an example, suffering the vengeance of eternal fire.' "

Bliss could almost smell the stench of Hades as the fire-and-brimstone preacher went on.

"I leave you today with one charge—that you not be fooled by those who have begun with God's grace in hand." Heath's pale eyes gleamed and the timbre of his voice grew stronger. "Look beyond the outer man and see what is in his heart. Turn away from the fornicator who with his chicanery may lead you along his evil path." Slowly he spread his arms wide and tilted his head back while his voice rose dramatically in volume. "Deny the silver-haired, silver-tongued devil in our midst lest he inveigle you to suffer the Almighty's vengeance in the next life."

Arden Heath gave her the creeps. She turned off the television. Trying to compare him to Osmond Wright was like comparing night to day. The preacher was almost manic. Or very, very clever. Again, Heath had referred to Osmond as the "silver-haired, silver-tongued devil in our midst." He'd intimated wrongdoing and payment.

*Do unto others* . . .

Did Heath have reason to hate Osmond other than his being a competitor? She hadn't had reason to connect him to her sister's disappearance before finding the note. Who better to quote the Bible? Logan had said the man who attacked her had little or light hair.

Bliss backed off and told herself to settle down. She was fabricating here. There was no way she could connect Melody to a televangelist who operated out of an adjoining state.

Or was there?

## Chapter Seven

Only half-awake the next morning, Bliss forgot about covering her neck until she checked herself in the mirror directly before leaving the apartment. There was no way she could camouflage the bruises considering she was wearing a scoop-necked blouse. She made a quick change into the one dress she'd brought with a stand-up collar, then drove her car over to the other side of the compound so she wouldn't be late for work again. She was trying to act casual as she entered the office.

Already at her desk, Hope looked up. "Morning. Before you sit down our financial director has a problem."

Bliss froze. "Problem?"

She hoped the word came out naturally; inside she was trying not to panic. Surely no one had found out she and Logan had been in the offices the night before. She was positive they'd put everything back in place.

"Susan had to take the morning off for an emergency dental appointment and Gregory needs someone to cover for her. I volunteered you. I hope you don't mind."

"Not at all." Relief poured through Bliss, relaxing her. "Doing something different keeps life interesting."

"Right." Hope gave her an odd look before going back to her paperwork.

"Uh, should I just go over there and introduce myself or what?"

The other woman didn't look up again. "Gregory isn't there at the moment, but he said he would be in before lunch. Make yourself at home at Susan's desk."

"Sure."

As she crossed the hall to the other office, Bliss wondered why Hope had seemed so...distant. Not unfriendly, exactly, but certainly different than she'd been the morning before when she'd brought over the surprise breakfast. Maybe she'd had a bad night or a fight with her husband. Or maybe this was just her office personality. Hope hadn't made any other friendly overtures the day before, though Bliss had been too busy to think about it until now.

She was kept almost as busy as she'd been on Monday when she'd covered for Susan during her break. No sooner had she transferred one call or taken a message than the telephone rang again. Until halfway through the morning when the calls slacked off, she had little time to think about her reasons for being there.

Not that she could make sense of anything she'd learned to date. There were too many missing pieces to the puzzle. She supposed she could ask Logan whether his father and Heath had any kind of personal vendetta going, but she didn't have the faintest idea about what to look for next. And even if she learned Heath and Osmond had more reason than competitiveness to hate each other, Bliss didn't want to tell Logan about the note she'd found unless she had to.

Why was she so concerned about his feelings? Getting emotionally involved with him would be a big mistake. She believed his claim that he'd never been serious about Melody, but what about her sister's feelings.

And beyond her devotion to her sister were Logan's loyalties to the people he loved, especially his father. Most important was their conflict over the ministry itself. Bliss could never make this her way of life.

Startled by the thought, which made her attraction to Logan seem even more serious than she'd realized, she was further frustrated when the telephone rang again. She picked up the receiver with a jerk and took a calming breath before answering.

"Osmond Wright Ministry Financial Offices."

"Let me speak to Townsend."

The guttural voice issuing the demand was neither pleasant nor natural sounding, as if the speaker were trying to disguise his identity.

"I'm sorry," Bliss said. "But Mr. Townsend isn't in at the moment—"

"Don't try to stall me, Susie."

"I'm not—"

"Tell him *the man* is getting impatient. He wants to complete the transaction and soon."

"I beg your pardon?"

"Just give him the message."

Although she figured she wouldn't get an answer, Bliss still asked, "Who should I say is calling?"

After the line went dead, she stared at the receiver a moment before hanging up. Whoever the man was, he'd thought she was Susan. Was that why he hadn't left a name, because Gregory Townsend's secretary would have known who he was? Or could something more sinister be going on? He'd made it sound as if Townsend owed money to someone important.

Despite Logan's assurances that the financial director was loyal to his father, did he have some reason to bilk the ministry of funds...and to be involved with men who were potentially dangerous, perhaps not only to him but to Melody and herself as well?

"IT TOOK YOU LONG ENOUGH."

The man ground out the words to establish rank. While he hadn't come up with the plan, he would use what was freely offered and make the most of the opportunity. Taking advantage of others' weaknesses had always been his specialty. He'd been born with the ability to milk a con for all it was worth.

Frowning, his partner said, "I got here as soon as I could."

"So what the hell is going on?"

"Nothing good."

"Meaning?"

"We'll have to speed up the denouement."

"The singing angel still poking her nose around?"

"Not only is Bliss after us, but now she has Logan on her side."

"You're sure about that?" the man asked.

"Positive, and it's making me nervous. If either one of them stumbles onto something that'll lead them to us, there's going to be hell to pay—"

"I'll take care of it."

"Let me make this clear—I want them temporarily derailed, not dead."

"Especially not Logan, right?"

"Neither of them." With an alarmed expression, his partner asked, "What kind of a monster do you think I am? Murder wasn't part of the deal."

"Sometimes deals change."

The man savored the fact that his taunting worked. He wanted to keep the upper hand. While he wasn't adverse to opposing the law—not even if it meant violence—

murder was a crime without a statute of limitations. Then again, he would do what he had to. He was going to walk away from this situation a winner.

Besides, if something went wrong, he didn't have to be the one to take the fall. . . .

JOELLE MACKEY sat behind the wheel of her long, white Cadillac, Bliss keeping her company in the passenger seat. They progressed through the residential section of Wrightville slowly, as though Joelle wanted to make her presence known. At least that's the impression Bliss got when the woman waved regally to an old man sitting in a rocking chair on the front porch of a neat little clapboard house.

"Mr. Peterson!" she called to the senior citizen.

The man tipped his hat respectfully and kept rocking.

Bliss stared at the oddity on his porch. "What is that decoration? A swan?"

"Now that's a cement goose, Bliss, darlin'. At least every other porch in this neck of the woods has one. Not just Wrightville, but the surrounding towns as well. Some people buy pairs—so one doesn't get lonely, I guess."

A glance at the houses on her side of the street confirmed that observation. "I don't believe this," Bliss said, her lips quirking. She'd been too stressed the last time she'd driven through town to notice. "They're all wearing different outfits. Aprons and bonnets, vests and caps."

"It's a strange tradition," Joelle explained. "The geese are dressed according to the weather or season. If it ever rains, they'll all wear their little yellow vinyl sou'westers. And then there's the holidays. Ghosts, goblins and witches for Halloween, and at Christmas, Santas, elves and reindeer geese."

The wind picked up and cloth danced around the geese making them look as if they were about to fly. Bliss laughed out loud and Joelle joined her. It was the first really unguarded moment they'd shared. Since leaving the compound, Joelle had seemed as wary of Bliss as she had of the redhead.

"It is silly," Bliss admitted once she regained control of herself. "But it's kind of cute."

"Try eccentric."

The sarcasm was back, as if Logan's aunt didn't want to be thought sentimental about the town. Bliss couldn't tell if the older woman liked Wrightville or not, and the same went for Joelle's attitude toward her brother-in-law "Ossie." Bliss wondered how the preacher reacted to an undignified nickname that could be interpreted either as affectionate or caustic. No doubt he was used to his sister-in-law's moods and undisciplined tongue.

Joelle reached for a cigarette, her third since they'd left the ministry grounds barely ten minutes before. Bliss was to help her run errands, both business and personal, for the entire family. Joelle insisted she had a list an arm long and had come to Hope for help. Since her daughter-in-law had taken a late lunch and hadn't yet reappeared in the office, she'd drafted Bliss, who hadn't minded leaving the boring job of stuffing envelopes, especially since she could pick up some groceries before they headed back.

As an added bonus, she could both familiarize herself with the town... and with her companion. Who knew what information either could provide?

Joelle honked at an elderly woman in a swing on the porch of her white elephant of a house, which sat across from the quaint general store. "Mrs. Donnelly, how are you?" she called out.

"Doin' good, could be better."

"You take care now." To Bliss, Joelle said, "It never hurts to keep up goodwill with the citizens. We're the closest thing they have to royalty around here."

Bliss murmured, "I never thought of it that way."

"You ought to. Ossie put life back into this hick farm town. This place was economically depressed, on the verge of dying when he brought his ministry here. He drew new blood into the town and he's the main industry keeping these people employed. Some work for the ministry, others get the benefit of feeding or selling souvenirs to the tourists who pass through on their way to the compound."

"Then this wasn't always Wrightville?"

"Nope. But it has been as long as I've lived here." She crushed what was left of her cigarette into the ashtray. "I don't even remember what it used to be called."

"Do you have a specific job within the ministry?" Bliss asked.

Joelle turned the car onto Main Street. "Not really. I do a little of this, a little of that. All the unimportant things no one else wants to do, like going to the post office or the office-supply store or running personal errands. Everyone else is too busy to do those tasks, so they turn them over to me."

Bliss thought the other woman sounded bitter, as if she felt left out. "I would imagine you've been a great help to Dean's career, though."

Joelle laughed. "As if he appreciated my experience or advice. Dean hasn't listened to me in years. He thinks his mama is an interfering and peculiar character."

What a strange thing to say about herself. Bliss didn't have time to call up a line of questioning, however, for Joelle had turned into a diagonal parking spot in front of the post office at the town's center. Kitty-corner from them stood the dignified buff-colored courthouse with its manicured lawns on which was parked a tank, a souvenir of World War I. Removing the keys from the ignition, Joelle got out of the car and indicated Bliss should do likewise.

"We'll start at the post office," she stated, heading for the rear of the car. "Not only does the postage meter have to be updated, but the trunk is loaded with boxes of personal responses to members of Ossie's congregation."

"He answers them himself?"

"Ossie?" Joelle laughed, the sound acerbic. "No, darlin'. He's too busy supervising the entire operation instead of letting Dean take over more of the responsibility as he should be doing. Lurlene writes the letters. People get *her* advice, whether or not it makes any sense. But Ossie does sign the letters himself. Using a rubber stamp would be a tad too tacky, even for him."

Without waiting for a reply, Joelle reached into the trunk and lifted several open-topped boxes that were stacked together. Bliss did the same and followed the older woman into the post office. Several trips later, while Joelle waited inside as the clerk took care of the meter, Bliss went back to the car for the last batch.

She couldn't help thinking about the woman's odd attitude toward the ministry, Osmond and even Lurlene. If she didn't like her life or the people who surrounded her, why had she stayed in Wrightville for so long?

Money—the answer immediately came to Bliss. Joelle probably had no means of supporting herself in the style to which she'd become accustomed. She could get a job, though if she weren't entrusted with responsibility within the ministry, Bliss didn't know what kind of work the older woman could get outside. Or Dean might send her money, though with Osmond running the show, that might not amount to much.

Bliss stacked the last few boxes together. One was half empty and contained personal mail. She placed it on top, but as she lifted the stack, the wind gusted and dumped the contents into the trunk's interior.

A few of the envelopes flew to the back of the trunk and Bliss had to climb up onto the bumper to reach them. She was so exasperated with herself that she almost missed the dove-gray envelope in the midst of a half-dozen others. As she slid back to the ground and re-stacked the mail into the box, the significance of the familiar stationery struck her. She quickly lifted the envelope. She'd barely noted the flowing handwriting and that no name accompanied the ministry's returned address when she realized Joelle was exiting the post office with the meter.

Bliss quickly placed the envelope at the end of the stack. She hadn't seen to whom the letter was addressed, but she knew it was on its way to a box office number registered in Louisville, Kentucky. Maybe she could get another peek at it once inside the post office.

That hope was dashed when Joelle said, "I'll take the last pile." She placed the meter in the trunk and took the boxes. "I'll be right back and we can start working on the rest of the list."

Tucking her frustration away for the moment, Bliss smiled. "I'll be waiting."

Who had written the letter? If only she could find out, she would undoubtedly know the identity of the person who had sent that threat to Osmond. And would be one step closer to her sister. If she asked Joelle directly, she would raise the other woman's suspicions. What if the stationery belonged to her?

Bliss sighed and told herself to relax. Not a very easy task, but at least she could cover her building stress with a placid smile.

The newspaper office was next. Joelle introduced Bliss to the editor, then handed him new copy for the ministry's weekly ad. In return, he gave her a folder containing a dozen tear sheets of a recent article profiling Dean. Bliss made a mental note to read the copy as soon as possible. It wouldn't hurt to find out more about the young man who wanted to be Osmond's successor.

They made several more stops and trips back to the car before crossing the street to Eve's Sundries, what Joelle described as a drugstore–gift shop. She took a long list of personal items from her handbag, tore it in half and handed one of the pieces to Bliss.

"We can each collect half the items and be finished twice as fast," Joelle told her.

"Fine with me. I want to make sure I have enough time to buy those groceries."

"Don't worry, we'll get to the general store and you'll make tonight's choir rehearsal with no problem."

Eve's Sundries fit its name. Every available space was packed with items. Checking her list, Bliss headed for the first-aid section where she found a box of Band-Aids. She was looking for the right size elastic wrap when a familiar voice distracted her.

"Say, aren't you one of those famous Singing Angels? Can I have your autograph?"

Bliss turned around. "Erma Dixon, what are you doing here?"

"My sister, Eve, owns the place." Erma lowered her voice conspiratorially. "She employs me, though she says I'm about as much help as a possum in a chicken coop."

Their combined laughter made Bliss feel better than she had since she'd discovered the letter. Then it was Erma's turn to question her.

"What are you doing here? I thought you told me you were working for the ministry stuffing envelopes."

"Today's been a real treat," Bliss said with a grin. "I answered phones in the finance office this morning, and now I'm helping Joelle Mackey shop." She indicated her list. "I'd probably better get busy."

"Let me help you."

With Erma's guidance around the crowded store, Bliss had her part of the list complete in no time. She placed the final item—a get well card—in her basket. As she was about to thank Erma, she noticed boxed paper and envelopes next to the card display. She scanned the shelves, which were lined with flowery stationery. No gray watermark bond.

"Looking for a specific pattern?" Erma asked.

"Something plain. Gray, if you have it."

"We don't carry anything that elegant. Try the office-supply store on the next block."

If only she had the time. "Thanks for your help. See you tonight."

Bliss headed for the front of the store, but even without assistance, Joelle had beaten her to the register. The other woman was unloading her basket on the counter.

Eve began sorting through the items, checking the price tags. "Find everything you need?"

Joelle checked her list. "All but one item. You're out of Laviana Rose Water."

"Wait a minute. Our distributor made a delivery this morning. Erma," she called loudly, "see if there's any rose water in that new shipment."

Bliss emptied the contents of her basket behind the others, and Eve began totaling the items. Before she'd finished, her sister appeared, waving a porcelain bottle decorated with white roses.

"Is this what you're looking for, Mrs. Mackey?"

"That's it," Joelle agreed.

Eve took the rose water from her sister and totaled the bill, which Joelle then signed before Bliss could get a good look at the handwriting.

"Always a pleasure to do business with you, Mrs. Mackey," Eve said. "You have a good evening now."

"I intend to."

"One last stop," Joelle announced as they added the purchases to the growing mass in the trunk. "And then we're on our way home."

And to rehearsal, Bliss thought, wishing she could just make herself dinner and go to sleep. Exhaustion was already setting in from a lack of sleep.

When they pulled up in front of the general store, with its old red gas pumps that were straight out of the fifties, Bliss was sure her tired eyes were playing tricks on her. It wasn't the setting itself that took her aback, nor the billboard advertising *The Osmond Wright Workaday Bible*, but the black Lincoln and the man who got out and disappeared around the left side of the building.

He looked oddly familiar, even with that brimmed hat pulled low over his eyes.

"You go in and get your groceries. I'll make sure this beast gets fed," Joelle said of the Cadillac.

The wind was so brisk that Bliss had to hold her skirt in place as she crossed the pavement to the general store. Once inside, she forgot about the man while she took the opportunity to call Indianapolis. She informed her business partner that, since she hadn't yet learned what happened to her sister, she would be gone longer than she'd expected.

Gathering several days' worth of groceries, she brought them to the counter and looked out the window. The attendant was now checking the engine oil. Oddly enough, Joelle was nowhere to be seen. Perhaps the inveterate chain-smoker had been desperate for a cigarette and had wandered away from the volatile pump fumes.

But when Bliss exited the store and looked around, she still didn't see the other woman. The attendant was just closing the hood.

"Have you seen Mrs. Mackey?" she asked.

The young man wiped grease from his hands with a paper towel. "No, ma'am. I thought she followed you inside."

"She didn't. How strange."

"What's strange?"

Bliss turned as Joelle approached them, obviously having come from around the back of the building.

"I was just wondering where you'd disappeared to," Bliss told her.

"Why, I had to stop in the little girls' room."

"Oh."

Feeling foolish, Bliss set the groceries on the rear seat and climbed into the car while Joelle paid the attendant. It wasn't until the other woman was behind the wheel, turning the car around the lot in a wide circle, that the man in the brimmed hat strolled out into the open from the shadows of the store.

This time, she got an even better look at his face. "That's him!"

"Him who?"

"Arden Heath." Bliss craned around to get one last look at the man as he climbed into the black Lincoln. The wind flipped off his hat and she got a glimpse of a bald head. "Take a look."

Joelle glanced over her shoulder, but the man was already inside the car. "You must be mistaken, darlin'," she said, turning onto Main Street. "He lives in Kentucky, not around here. Besides, The Reverend Arden Heath is one of Ossie's oldest enemies. He wouldn't be caught dead here in Wrightville."

*Enemies.*

Although she was tempted to ask Joelle why she'd chosen that word rather than competitors, she held her tongue. But that didn't stop her from wondering, not only about the enmity between the two men or about why Heath might have chosen to visit Wrightville, but about what Joelle had really been doing while Bliss had been grocery shopping.

She told herself to slow down. Her imagination was running on full, fueled by the note she'd found in her sister's Bible.

Immersed in her own ruminations, Bliss barely responded to Joelle's running commentary on their return trip to the compound. She went on and on in a friendly manner, while Bliss became more and more morose about the mess she seemed to have placed herself in.

Melody had disappeared five days before. Would she ever make sense of the clues and impressions she'd been storing away bit by bit? She didn't want to hurt Logan and show him the note addressed to his father. And with Joelle assuring her that Arden Heath wouldn't be caught dead in Wrightville, she had to wonder if she could trust her own powers of observation.

Still, Bliss was convinced that her eyes hadn't deceived her and wanted Logan's opinion on the matter. Since she would have to help Joelle unload the trunk and get the groceries into her own place, she didn't know when she would catch up with him. At least she would have plenty of time to prepare and eat dinner, maybe rest for a while, before going to rehearsal.

A half hour later, while unloading her groceries onto her kitchen counter, Bliss glanced out the window. She noticed a figure she would have sworn was Logan heading north across the rise of the hill in the direction of the natural springs. Unsure what he was up to, she decided to seize the opportunity to interrupt him.

She could reiterate the baffling telephone message she'd taken for Townsend, who'd never returned to his office. And she could describe the mysterious stranger she'd seen in town. She was sure that Logan wouldn't mind being distracted from his purpose for a good reason. Her excitement at catching up with him was due only to sharing new information; there was nothing personal in the accelerated rhythm of her pulse.

Gathering the food on the counter, she put it all into the refrigerator, then grabbed her purse and ran to her car, which was parked in the apartment-complex lot.

If nothing else, Logan could tell her about the feud between his father and Arden Heath and she might begin to make sense of the warnings that had been televised . . . not to mention the one still hidden in Melody's Bible.

AS HE APPROACHED the natural-springs area, Logan slowed down to catch his breath. The final preparations to the landscaping were only now being made in anticipation of the season's first paying guests who were to arrive that weekend. The rich smell of new-mown grass pleasantly teased his nose, and the beauty of the wooded area around the ponds assuaged his growing apprehension.

He hated to think that Bliss had found something disturbing in this tranquil haven. Finding her note on his desk had come as a surprise—so had her request that he meet her in the pool house as soon as possible. The missive had held a sense of urgency he couldn't ignore. Had she found something belonging to Melody in there?

Surely not anything indicating violence....

The door to the pool house was open. The interior lay in darkness except for faint shafts of fading light spilling through the west windows.

"Bliss?"

The acoustics of the high-ceilinged room added to the water from the springs that constantly cycled through the pool made his voice sound strangely hollow. An unexpected premonition bristled the hair on the back of his neck. What was wrong? He concentrated his senses on his surroundings. If something had happened to...

"Bliss, where are you?" he called louder.

No answer.

Logan took several steps forward and stopped less than a yard from the pool. He squinted as if that would help him pierce the gloom of the cavernous interior, but he saw nothing. He wasn't sure if instinct warned him or if he actually heard a sound that made him turn to his right.

A flash of movement that sprang out of the dark preceded a glancing blow to his head.

His vision blurred with the onset of pain. He wavered unsteadily, shook his head to clear it, but his surroundings spun faster and faster. His fleeting impression of a dark-garbed figure was interrupted by strong hands shoving him off balance. Suddenly water was rising toward him and he couldn't stop it, couldn't stop himself. And then he was wrapped in its suffocating wet grip.

God have mercy on his soul, for he was about to black out and there wasn't a damn thing he could do to save himself from drowning.

## Chapter Eight

Bliss crested the hilly road just as Logan vanished around the corner of what she assumed was the building housing the spring-fed swimming pool Hope had told her about. She swung her car onto the road leading down to the empty parking lot next to the long, gray structure. The pool house had been built on the bank overlooking one of the ponds. Adding to the tranquil scene were small cabins peeking out from between wooded areas surrounding the water.

She didn't sense anything was wrong until she left the car near the pool house. A muffled sound made her pause midstride. Her brow furrowed as she listened intently, but no other noise split the silence.

"Logan?" she cried, not caring who might be in the vicinity to hear.

When he didn't answer it frightened Bliss and made her flesh crawl. Sure that he had disappeared inside the building, she rushed forward. Instinct prompted her to look for a weapon of some kind, but there wasn't even a loose branch around. The grounds keepers had apparently been diligent in their spring-cleanup work. As she was about to continue inside unarmed, she spotted a tool left in the newly planted flower beds. Picking up the claw-shaped device used for loosening earth, she gripped its handle tightly.

Then she entered the pool house.

Her unsteady breathing sounded distorted and amplified to her ears. Senses attuned to her surroundings, she held her breath as she slowly continued forward. Listening. Searching. The click of her heels echoed hollowly through the high-ceilinged room. Nerves taut, heart in her throat, she stopped, but heard only the steady trickle of water.

Then a burst of sound....

Whipping around, she slashed out with all her might, her weapon catching her attacker by surprise before he could touch her. He grunted in pain and whirled away, denying her a glimpse of the face beneath the knit stocking cap, which he pulled even lower over his brow.

"Logan, are you in here?" she cried, backing away from her assailant, staring at him as her eyes adjusted to the gloom. He almost blended into his murky surroundings, was almost at one with the shadows. "What did you do to Logan?"

He didn't answer—not that she'd expected him to.

Bliss gripped the tool, ignoring the unnatural rushing sound inside her head, and propped up her courage. "Get the hell out of here or I'll scream loud enough so they hear me at the parsonage."

Her bluff didn't work. Head down, the man advanced on her, his next strike so quick and hard that he temporarily paralyzed her arm and sent the gardener's tool spinning through the air. Panicked, and trying to get away from him, she dodged to the side. Her heel caught on the pool's lip and she stumbled and lost her balance. Her other foot met thin air....

With a wail of surprise, she went tumbling backward into the pool. By the time she came up sputtering, the sound of leather slapping against cement, followed by a door slamming, bounced from wall to wall. Her attacker had fled. Relieved, she treaded water and tried to catch her breath.

Then something nudged her—something long and solid.

An arm floated around her waist.

She screamed and thrashed so hard that she swallowed a mouthful of water before she managed to regain control and realize there was no threat. Spitting out water and blinking hard, she stared at the floating body... and recognized the victim.

"Logan!"

Clawing at his clothing, Bliss turned him face up. She grabbed a handful of curly hair and tried to check his vital signs. His skin was clammy and his pulse so weak that it was almost nonexistent. She put her cheek to his mouth but couldn't tell if he was breathing.

Luckily her small size wasn't inhibiting in the water. She easily pulled Logan to the shallow end of the pool, using her body to secure him head up against the ledge. The skirt of her dress floated to the surface of the water and billowed around her like a parachute.

How to get him out of the water and onto a horizontal surface to administer lifesaving techniques was the question. If she couldn't get Logan out of the pool, she would have to work on him as best she could right where they were. She smacked her open hand against his stomach hoping it would force any water from his lungs. The method didn't work. She pushed her hand against his chest to keep him pinned against the wall while she repositioned herself over him and pulled his head back.

"You're going to breathe if I have to do it for you," she muttered, struggling with his weight because they were now both half in, half out of the water. "Even I'm not quite sure how this is done."

Bliss took a deep breath, placed her mouth over his and expelled her air into him slowly. She swore she felt his heartbeat quicken under the hand pressing against his chest. Encouraged, she tilted her head away, took another breath and turned back to him. This time, she felt as if he were taking the air from her.

She'd done it! He was alive!

"Logan, are you all right?"

"I will be . . . in a minute."

He was breathing hard and she could feel the hammering of his heart. But he was also hugging her and the closeness made her uncomfortable.

Bliss freed herself and waded over to the steps. Climbing them, she realized she'd lost a shoe somewhere in the pool. "Darned heels," she muttered.

Wondering how she was going to find her shoe in deep water when it was semidark, she managed to ignore Logan until he started to follow her. He didn't get far before he groaned loudly and stopped.

"What's wrong?" she asked.

"Just trying to move. My head feels like someone clubbed it." He put his hand to his temple and winced. "Maybe that's because someone did."

Once more he edged toward the steps but quickly stopped and hung on to the ledge as if to steady himself.

Unable to allay her suspicions, she asked, "You're not putting me on, are you?"

"Yeah." He turned to face her and almost managed to suppress another groan. "I'm having a laugh a minute in here."

She removed the remaining shoe and dropped it to the cement walk before slipping back into the water. "I'll help you."

"Thanks."

Bliss waded toward him. "What happened, anyway?" she asked, slipping her arm around his waist.

"I was hoping you could answer that. Where were you?"

"Me? In town running errands with Joelle."

"When were you planning on getting here?" he demanded in a rising tone.

"You came here to meet *me*?"

"You indicated it was urgent."

"Do you have a concussion or something?" Stopping Logan before he could manage to climb the first underwater stair, she held her hand as far from his face as she could. "How many fingers am I holding up?" When he merely stared down at her with a disgusted grimace, she said, "All right. I believe you thought I wanted you to meet me here." She helped him maneuver the first step, then the next. "Now tell me why."

"The note."

For a rash moment, she thought he knew about the threat to his father. Bending away from him as much to cover her reaction as to pick up her discarded shoe, Bliss realized he must have gotten a message supposedly from her.

"I didn't send you any note, but I guess someone else wanted to meet you real badly."

This time Logan's groan wasn't one of pain. "Boy, have I been suckered. I found this typed message—which I thought *you* left—on my desk right before quitting time. It said to meet you here because you found new evidence. The thing was signed with a very flowery *B*."

"In a way *you* discovered something new," she told him. "Whoever is on to me knows we're working together. And now we know we're both in danger." Suddenly she felt incredibly guilty. "Logan, I'm sorry I got you into this mess of mine. I didn't mean for you to get hurt."

"Getting hurt was my own fault."

He wrapped his hand around the back of her neck and gently massaged away the growing tension. If only he could assuage her conscience as easily. What if she hadn't seen him head this way? What if he'd been found dead in the pool? Slipping his hand down to her shoulder, making her turn into his chest and wrap her arms around his back, Logan continued walking and talking, comforting her when he was the one who'd been hurt.

"I should have been smart enough to know you wouldn't leave a message like that where anyone might find it. Besides, I volunteered to help you, remember?"

Bliss didn't feel like arguing the point. Logan was leaning on her again as they made their way to the door. His weight had lightened, as if he were more easily moving on his own. When her bare foot struck something solid, it was as if Fate was trying to equalize the pain.

"Ow!"

He stopped immediately. "What happened? Are you all right?"

"Just a few bruised toes." She scanned the area. "There it is—a piece of two-by-four. Look familiar?"

"I didn't exactly see it coming, but I suspect my skull would recognize it."

Bliss could neither miss Logan's ironic statement nor resist a smart retort. "You're right. I think I can just make out the dent your head made."

"Think you're funny, don't you, Smart—"

"Uh-uh. What kind of talk would that be from a preacher's son?"

"My father was the one who nicknamed me the black sheep, remember?" He tugged her into moving.

Ignoring the black sheep reference, she protested. "Wait a minute. Shouldn't we take that piece of wood for the fingerprints?"

"I think this guy was smart enough to wear gloves, don't you?"

"You've got a point."

Bliss registered that Logan was walking almost on his own now, though he didn't take his arm from her shoulders. She would have suggested he do so, but she was sure that would start another argument and she didn't have one left in her. She needed time to regroup.

Once outside, she kept an eye out for signs of the attacker, but she and Logan seemed to be alone.

"Whoever is taking care of that pool is going to be surprised at the strange objects he finds in the morning," she said. "A two-by-four. A shoe." She looked at the single ruined scrap of leather in her hand and wondered why she'd bothered taking it. "And a gardening tool."

"Gardening tool?"

"One of those clawlike things. Not a bad weapon. It might have saved both our lives. I got the sucker with it before he made me fall into the pool."

Logan stopped her in midstride halfway across the parking lot. "Are you saying you actually wounded him?"

"Yes—I mean he acted like I hurt him some, not that it stopped him."

"That's great."

Frowning up at him, Bliss shivered. "It was disgusting. I've never hurt another human being in my life. I was only trying to protect myself."

"I don't condone violence. I meant that if you wounded him, we might be able to figure out who he was. Where did you hit him?"

"I—I'm not sure."

Her mood subtly changed as she once more confronted what might have happened—and thought about what she was still keeping from him. She was going to have to find a way to tell him about the threat to his father. Arguing with Logan and joking with him had been ways to put off reality for a few moments, but now it came crashing back on her full force, especially when he persisted in questioning her.

"Where do you think you wounded this guy?"

Bliss shrugged. "The arm, maybe. Or the chest. I just whacked out at him blindly." She stared up at Logan. His temple was starting to swell and discolor. "I haven't been thinking straight. We're going around and around about something we can't do anything about right now, while I should be driving you to the nearest hospital."

"That's a half hour away." He started walking toward her car on his own. "Forget it."

Bliss rushed after him. Seeing fresh blood mixed in his dark curls, she raised a hand as if to touch him there but caught herself before causing him more physical pain.

"I'll take you to a doctor, then."

"I don't need one."

"You're bleeding."

Without breaking his stride, Logan steeled his face into a mask and ran his fingers through his curls. The skin around his eyes tightened when he touched his head and his fingertips came away bright red.

"You see. You need a doctor."

"This is nothing," he protested, stopping when he got to her Ford. "A scalp wound."

"You don't know that." She whipped past him and opened the passenger door. "Get in. I'm taking you to a doctor or the nearest medical person around here and I don't want any arguments from you!"

"All right." Logan carefully slid into the passenger seat. "You win. To the apartment complex, then."

"There's a doctor living at the ministry?"

"Not exactly, but the next best thing—a ministering angel. You."

"You're crazy. You could have a concussion and might need stitches."

"I promise to lie down on your couch . . . or your bed, if you prefer," he said, grinning up at her wickedly. "And you can lavish all the tender, loving care on me that you obviously think I need."

"Logan—"

He placed a hand over her mouth, effectively stopping her argument. She sighed. It was no use. Maybe he really was so hardheaded that the blow hadn't affected him at all.

"Deal?" he asked, removing his hand.

"Deal. I just hope no one comes looking for me and finds you in such a mess. Rehearsal," she explained, closing the passenger door and circling the vehicle. "I'm developing a bad habit here. I'm going to be late."

When she slid behind the wheel, he covered her hand with his before she could put the key into the ignition. He made her look at him. His gray eyes were filled with an emotion that confused her.

"You weren't too late for *me*," he said. "You saved my life."

"As you saved mine."

Caught for a moment by invisible threads that inexplicably bound them together, she broke the connection when she turned away and started the car. This was no time to be falling for a man, even if she and Logan were right for each other—which they weren't. From now on, they were both going to have to work harder to find Melody.

And they were going to have to watch their backs if they wanted to come out of this alive.

"YOU'RE GOING TO BE A MESS in the morning, but unless you pretend a sudden fetish for hats, you're not going to be able to hide the bruising."

"I'll think of some explanation. *Ahh!*"

Sitting on the toilet seat, prey to her ministering hands, Logan clenched his jaw against the pain Bliss was causing him as she used a gauze wipe laced with hydrogen peroxide to clean out the cut. He'd thought himself lucky when they'd discovered the medicine cabinet still contained all the basics.

"What kind of explanation?"

"Let's see." He was trying to keep his sense of humor, but the fiery sensation added to the pounding in his head was making that difficult. "I could say I was driving down the gravel road to my place too fast and the front tire whipped up a rock that hit me in the head."

"Tch, tch. Adding lies to bad language."

"At least my vices are innocent."

"I doubt that," Bliss mumbled, turning away and dumping the gauze pad in the trash and rearranging the first-aid kit. Anything so she didn't have to look at him.

Logan wished she would talk openly about her feelings concerning him with as much honesty as she used when discussing other subjects—like his father's ministry. He knew she was confused, but he could deal with that. Even if she fought the closeness he wanted, he knew she wasn't immune to him any more than he was to her.

"Maybe I should bandage the cut," Bliss said.

"Why? It's not bleeding again, is it?"

"Not really, but it could get infected."

"I'll take my chances. What I really could use is a couple of extrastrength aspirins."

"Coming right up."

She stood to replace the first-aid kit in the medicine cabinet. Her blue cotton dress was drying rapidly, but damp spots still clung to her delectable form. Heaven knew, he wasn't meant to be a monk. Not that he went from woman to woman just because he had a need to prove his sexual prowess. Thanks to his upbringing, he had to have special feelings for a woman before making love to her. And there had only been a few such women in his life—one of whom had not been Bliss's sister.

Melody. She was part of the problem. Logan wanted to get to know Bliss better, to get close to her without her sister or his father's calling coming between them.

"Here it is." Bliss popped the cap off the aspirin bottle and shook out two tablets. She handed them to him with a glass of water.

"You're a lifesaver. Thanks."

"You already thanked me," she said. "And I thanked you. If we're not careful, we're going to turn into a mutual admiration society."

"Would that be such a bad idea?"

"Yes."

"Why?"

Obviously intending to ignore the question, she leaned back against the sink and changed the subject. "You never asked me why I came after you earlier."

"I'll bite—anywhere you want."

That she ignored his teasing sent a strange feeling through Logan's gut. She seemed . . . nervous.

"A couple of things happened today that I thought you should know about," she continued. "I took a message for Gregory Townsend this morning from some guy who wouldn't identify himself. Very strange. He said 'the man' was getting impatient and wanted to complete the transaction. He wouldn't explain further."

Relief washed through Logan. He'd thought she was going to point the finger closer to home. "So Gregory got a strange phone call."

"It sounded like your financial director owed money he didn't have. What if Townsend's the one who's been depleting the ministry? And that isn't all. I'm sure I saw Arden Heath in town today."

That information startled Logan. "Heath? Are you sure?"

"As sure as I can be, though Joelle tried to tell me I was wrong."

"Did she see the man?"

"No. At least I don't think so. But she said he wouldn't be caught dead in town because he was one of your father's oldest enemies. What did she mean by that?"

"They're rivals for the same spiritual congregation."

Bliss studied him intently, making Logan uncomfortable again. There was a lot more to the enmity between the two men and he sensed she knew it.

"They're not exactly vying for the same type of people from what I've seen," she said. "The truth. Please. This may be important."

Though he didn't know how Heath's quarrel with his father could be connected to Melody or to the missing funds, Logan decided to appease her with the whole sordid story.

"This goes way back, to when I was a kid. We were still living in Louisville. A young woman—one of Heath's followers—came to my father for help. She claimed Heath had seduced her, had gotten her pregnant and had brought her to a doctor for a supposed checkup. What she got instead was an abortion. An illegal one done without her knowledge or consent. She didn't realize what was happening to her until it was over."

"Good Lord," Bliss whispered. "How awful. What did your father do?"

"He sent her to a doctor in our congregation who examined the woman and agreed that she had had a recent abortion. A friend confirmed there had been an affair between the woman and Heath. Then father went to the church board and demanded an investigation."

"Did they agree to act?"

He nodded. "There was a hearing. Under great duress, Heath confessed to his illicit relationship with the young woman, claiming that he had been the one wronged, that she had seduced him. For good measure, he added that she'd sworn revenge when he'd broken off the relationship because he'd seen the error of his ways. He cried through his entire testimony."

Logan told the story calmly, though he remembered the turmoil that had upset his own household at the time. For some reason, his mother hadn't wanted her husband involved in the matter. He hadn't been able to understand her unusual attitude then. And when he'd had the facts reiterated to him as an adult, he'd been equally disturbed that his mother who was usually so warm and caring about others had seemed so cool and callous at the time.

"Anyway," Logan continued, "Heath testified that the young woman had been very experienced and might have been with any number of men before and after him. He denied knowledge of a pregnancy or abortion. She couldn't prove he was involved. The doctor couldn't be found to corroborate her story."

"So Heath got away with it?" Bliss asked, sounding horrified.

"With the pregnancy and abortion part, yes. But because he admitted to the relationship with a member of his flock, Heath was barred from the ministry for six months. During that time, the members of his congregation turned away from him and prevented him from coming back. I'm sure they were wondering whose daughter might end up on the scandal sheets next. So Heath had to start over. He changed his image and found a new segment of the population who responded to it. He made what you might call a transformation into the man you see now."

"This certainly sheds light on his hatred for your father."

"Especially since the board of The Congregation of the Lord allotted extra funds for Osmond Wright to expand here in Indiana, soon after the infamous episode."

"A reward of sorts."

"It wasn't, but Heath saw it that way. He swore revenge on my father, but he's never carried through with the threat."

"I'm not so sure about that."

The uneasy feeling returned. "Why do you say that?" Logan asked.

A silent and very serious-looking Bliss moved away from the sink to the linen closet. She reached inside behind the stack of towels and pulled out a book. When she came closer, Logan recognized Melody's Bible.

"You have to understand why I didn't show this to you when I found it last night." She avoided his eyes as she flipped through the pages, then pulled out a folded piece of paper. "I knew how upset you would be, and I couldn't figure out how this fit in with my sister's disappearance, so I kept it to myself."

"I suspected you'd found something."

Logan took the paper, unfolded it and with as much calm as he could maintain, read the threat to his father that began with a quotation from the Bible.

"What is going on here?" Adrenaline sluicing through him, he looked up at Bliss who was staring at him, her eyes troubled. Hurt, he struck out at her. "You would have shared this information if you really trusted me."

"Trust has nothing to do with this. I just didn't want you to be hurt. That's all."

He heard the truth of her words and forced himself to calm down. "Why should I be angry at you when my own father couldn't even show this to me." He was beginning to understand why she'd felt the past could be so important. "You think Heath sent this to my father."

"I didn't have a clue when I found the note, but things are beginning to make some sense now." She took the note from him. "Remember the gray paper that caught in the wheel of your chair last night? I would have sworn it was the same as this. I figured the person issuing the threat was working from the inside. And then when I saw a letter written on the same stationery go out in the personal mail earlier today, I was convinced of a connection. I just couldn't figure out how the elements were related—Melody, the money, the threat.''

"But now you have?"

"Maybe." Bliss refolded the note and replaced it in the Bible, which she returned to its hiding place. "I hope I'm wrong, but . . ." Her voice seemed to give out on her, as if she were struggling not to cry. She hit the closet door with the flat of her hand and took a deep breath. "Your telling me about Heath made me put together a not-so-nice picture, one that I'm afraid neither of us is going to like."

Already guessing her suspicion, Logan agreed—he didn't like it one bit. "Go on."

"Heath was sexually involved with a young woman in his congregation. Osmond blew the whistle and Heath swore revenge." Bliss began to pace the narrow confines of the bathroom. "What if . . . if the rumors are true about my sister and your father and Heath found out about their affair. Think about the wording of the note. Do unto others . . . telling Osmond he'd be sorry he didn't look to his own sins. Arden Heath may very well be blackmailing your father who is in turn paying him off from ministry funds."

"I don't believe it," Logan said tightly, fighting his rising anger.

She stopped to face him. "And I don't *want* to believe it. Give me an alternative," she begged him.

"I don't have one. Yet." He rose and, since she was still barefoot, loomed over her. "Your theory isn't quite complete. It doesn't explain what happened to Melody."

"Maybe she did leave in disgrace . . . or to protect your father from further possible exposure."

Ignoring the light-headed feeling that made him a bit unsteady on his feet, he stepped closer. "Then why the attacks on the two of us? Why would someone want us dead?''

"I haven't figured that out!" Bliss cried, her voice rising with frustration.

"I thought you believed your sister was innocent of any wrongdoing."

"I don't know what to believe anymore. This whole scenario keeps getting more and more complex. Nothing is cut-and-dried. Nothing is simple."

"Then don't believe the worst about someone you love without having all the facts. Maybe you've put together part of the truth, but we have to keep digging and sorting to fill in the missing pieces. Until then, have faith. Sometimes it helps."

*And God helps those who help themselves.*

How many times had he heard his father say so? Logan wondered. If he'd been determined to get to the truth of the matter before, he was more bent on doing so now. With each day that passed, the stakes were getting higher. He only prayed that he and Bliss would find the facts before they paid with their lives.

THOUGH SHE WAS EMBARRASSED at being late for rehearsal, Bliss merely slipped into place and joined the rest of the choir in song. Thankfully it was a hymn she knew by heart. Now if only she could come up with some alternative answers for Logan, who had stretched out on her couch with the promise to continue the discussion when she returned.

Nothing new came to her so she soon gave up.

During a break between pieces, Erma signaled to her, indicating she wanted to talk later. Bliss nodded and went back to her sheet music.

Rehearsal ended promptly at ten. She and Erma moved toward each other.

"So what's up?" Bliss asked as they set out for the parking lot together.

"Nothing crucial. But you know that stationery you were looking for?"

Puzzled, Bliss said, "The gray bond."

"Well, I figured you were in a hurry, so I checked at the office-supply store for you. They don't have any in now, but they're expecting a shipment of supplies next week."

"Thanks. I'll keep that in mind."

"In the meantime, if you really need a few sheets you probably can get some."

Bliss felt her pulse pick up in tempo. "What do you mean?"

"The clerk said he sold the last box to someone right here at the ministry only a week ago."

"To whom?"

"Lurlene Wright. The store stocks it mainly for her."

A minute later, her thoughts in a muddle, Bliss got into her car and headed for the apartment complex. She'd been so sure Arden Heath had sent the threat to Osmond that she'd forgotten about the letter she'd seen that morning. Certainly the stationery was probably common enough to be purchased in any city, but what if...

No, the idea was too ridiculous. Lurlene couldn't be sending her own husband threatening notes. So why didn't she want to tell Logan about this new development? And how was she going to put on a front so that he wouldn't suspect she had something more to hide? Leaving the car in the lot, she approached her apartment with mounting trepidation.

But in the end, her dread was for naught.

Logan was gone.

LURLENE WRIGHT'S OFFICE was located at the rear of the parsonage overlooking the rose garden. She was alone at her desk, alone with her personal demons, trying to disregard them by keeping busy catching up on her correspondence. She felt as if she were being watched. Swiveling in her chair, she faced her son who was leaning against the door frame.

"Logan." Her heart pounded ridiculously. "My, you startled me. How long have you been standing there?"

"Only a minute."

He crossed the room and sat in the chair nearest her. Although he wasn't as big a man as his father, he looked equally uncomfortable when ensconced in the dainty furniture. About to ask him why he'd stopped by so late, Lurlene noticed the bruise that marred his temple.

"Logan, what happened to your head?"

"I ran into a door."

Lurlene's heart began to pound because of the lie. A mother knew if her son was telling the truth or not. She also knew when it was useless to press the issue.

"You should put some ice on it to stop the swelling."

"I didn't drop by to discuss me."

"Well, that sounds serious. Who do you want to talk about?"

"Father."

"Now, Logan," Lurlene began, trying to bluff. "You know I'm as worried about Osmond's health as you are, but I can't make him see—"

"Not his health."

Sensing what was coming, she forced a smile. "What, then?"

"We could begin with fifty thousand dollars missing from the treasury."

"Missing?"

"Don't act coy with me, Mother. You make it your business to know everything that goes on in the ministry."

Lurlene couldn't deny that. She was the woman behind the man, as the story of greatness went. She had always made sure Osmond's best interests were served, had always stood by him—even when he didn't deserve such undying loyalty. But she was a Southern lady, raised in a genteel world that didn't seem to exist any longer. The rules had changed. The problem was that she hadn't.

"Has your father mentioned this missing money?"

"No, as a matter of fact, he wouldn't discuss it with me. That's why I came to you."

"Leave it be. If your father isn't worried enough to share his problems with you, that means he has them under control. Besides, business matters are none of your concern."

"Even if Father wants me to take over the ministry?"

"You haven't agreed to that."

"No, but I have considered doing so."

He was trying to trick her into confiding in him. Logan didn't have the calling nor the nature to be his father's successor. She had always known that.

"I would advise you to talk things over with your father again, but that might upset him. He doesn't need any more stress."

"Especially not threats."

"What?"

Lurlene felt her heart go still for a moment, especially when she realized her son's eyes were pinned to her desk, to the letter she had been writing. When his gaze met hers, she could tell he was troubled.

"Logan, either say what's on your mind or say nothing. If you are trying to frighten me, you are succeeding."

"Would you tell me if someone threatened Father or would you expect me to ask him about that, too?"

Silence stretched between them and Lurlene felt as if her nerves were ready to snap. More and more, as the past caught up with them, she felt as though she'd been coasting out of control—an abhorrent, distasteful feeling. As if sensing she would reveal nothing he wanted to know, Logan rose. His expression was regretful.

"I'll be going now."

"You take care to put ice on that bruise."

Again he ignored the motherly advice. Without kissing her goodbye, he left the room. Tears sprang to her eyes, but she would not indulge herself. She had a stronger will hidden behind her gentle exterior than most people ever guessed. Logan had always been aware of that.

Lurlene took a deep, shuddering breath and wondered how much her son really knew.

## Chapter Nine

"Dean, baby, why don't you go ahead and tell your Uncle Ossie about your health spa idea," Joelle encouraged her son at lunch the next day.

"Mother, perhaps this is not the right time to bring up a new enterprise."

"No time ever seems to be right for this particular endeavor. You've been putting this conversation off for weeks now."

Dean flushed a deep red and glared at his mother but didn't argue the point. Bliss thought he looked younger than his years, despite the sophisticated style of his light red hair and the tailored three-piece suit that resembled his uncle's. A vulnerability shone in his dark brown eyes that she hadn't seen before. That, added to the things Logan had told her about his thwarted ambitions, made her heart go out to him.

"I think you should give it a go," Logan stated supportively. "I, for one, would like to hear what you have to say. Every business needs fresh ideas to keep it vital. This ministry is no different."

Her presence having been requested by Osmond himself as a goodwill gesture to a "promising novitiate" as he called her, Bliss glanced at the elder televangelist. He seemed to be ignoring Dean and his mother and concentrating on his food. In the meantime, Joelle was lighting a cigarette, despite the fact that everyone else was still eating. She was obviously agitated at her son's refusal to speak up for himself—and at Osmond's disinterested attitude.

Joelle planted her elbows on the creamy lace tablecloth, took a deep drag and insisted, "If you won't tell Ossie about your 'Healthy bodies house healthy souls' idea, I will."

"Concentrating on a new direction for the ministry would take more than a lunch hour," Lurlene interrupted. "Besides, discussing business in front of a guest would not be polite."

Logan's mother followed her statement with such an intense once-over of Bliss that it made her put down her silver fork. The delightful chicken salad with fresh fruits and chopped nuts suddenly lost its taste. She noticed that Hope had stopped eating as well. Her face expressionless, Dean's wife stared down into her plate.

"Yes, by all means, let us remain polite." Blue eyes cold, Joelle took an even deeper drag on the cigarette and aimed the smoke at the opposite end of the table as if she were purposely trying to aggravate Lurlene. "Bliss is square in the middle of the age group that a health spa idea would most appeal to. Besides, we could use a disinterested opinion here." She turned to the head of the table, and pointedly asked, "Don't you agree, Ossie?"

"Joelle, are you always going to be set on speechifying for your son?" Osmond asked, trading her question for question.

Before she could answer, Dean, who was seated between his uncle and Hope, cut in. "I can do my own talking, Uncle Osmond."

"Well?"

Joelle sank back against her chair and took a short puff before extinguishing her cigarette with several little jabs at her bread plate. Bliss took a sideways glance at Logan who sat next to his mother. His expression had become wary while Lurlene seemed outright displeased. She returned her attention to Osmond. Tension was rife before Dean even began.

"The health industry is one of the biggest in the world." Dean paused, as if to catch his breath now that he had the floor and all eyes were pinned on him. "Over the past dozen years, more and more people have become fitness conscious. They seek out diet and exercise programs tailored to their needs."

"There are thousands of places that can fill those needs all over this country," Osmond argued. "Why would you want to set one in the backwoods of Indiana?"

Dean seemed cowed into silence, and for a moment, Bliss thought he wouldn't find the resourcefulness to continue. He looked over at his wife and Hope lifted her eyes from the plate long enough to give him an encouraging smile. Then he recentered his attention on his uncle.

"The ministry could provide a program that takes care of the spiritual and the physical requirements of our members," Dean stated, gaining confidence and momentum. "So our facility would differ from the established health clubs and spas. We already have a modest beginning with the cottages and pool house surrounding the natural springs."

Bliss stiffened at the mention of the place where she and Logan might have lost their lives. She sneaked a look at Logan's swollen and bruised brow. He'd boldly lied to everyone, telling them he'd banged his head on a kitchen cabinet door.

"My idea is to expand the potential there," Dean went on.

"What? Add more cottages?"

"I see more cottages, a luxury inn with fully equipped spa facilities, a small chapel in the heart of the woods where participants can commune with nature and God. We can make this a year-round operation, with activities and spiritual seminars taking place both indoors and out."

"We don't have that kind of money to invest," Osmond said tersely.

Dean flushed again. "We can borrow the money, if necessary. This project will pay for itself."

"Or bankrupt us."

"Don't be so pessimistic, Ossie," Joelle said, her voice and posture indicating impatience and a growing anger with the man. "Dean's idea is a sure money-maker. Give him some credit, would you?"

"Mother—"

"We can play up the healing waters concept—"

"Those are natural springs," Lurlene cut in. "Not healing waters."

Joelle's face contorted in fury when she turned to the other woman. "For once in your life, stay out of my affairs!"

Lurlene threw her napkin on her plate and stood, almost knocking over her chair. Startled, Logan caught and steadied it. "Mother, please." He placed a hand on her arm, but she ignored him.

"*I* am Osmond's chosen partner in life and in his business. Please remember that."

"How could I ever forget with you around to remind me every moment, Lurlene, darlin'?" Joelle asked sweetly.

"Joelle, that was unnecessary!" Osmond shouted, then as his wife stalked away from the table toward the kitchen, added, "Lurlene, come back here!"

Now it was he who was turning red and throwing his napkin onto the table. Bliss thought he was about to have a stroke of apoplexy because Osmond was rubbing his left shoulder and chest.

"Uncle Osmond, please calm down," Dean pleaded. "We can discuss this at another time."

"There's nothing to discuss!"

Osmond rose and stormed into the kitchen after his wife. Bliss couldn't believe the startling turn of events, especially since the meal had started with such harmony. Only a few moments ago, Logan had teasingly nudged her foot under the table to get her attention and wink at her when no one was looking. Then at the snap of her fingers, the dynamics of the group had exploded and these people were at one another's throats.

Joelle was the next to stand. "I need a drink. Make that a half-dozen." She headed for the connecting living room and a cabinet with a drop leaf. "Make those doubles."

"Dean..." Hope began, her voice tapering off as her husband left the table as well.

"I'll talk to him," Logan volunteered.

Hope nodded and Logan went after his cousin. Only she and Bliss remained at the table. The clink of crystal on crystal caught Bliss's attention and she glanced into the next room where Joelle held a decanter in one hand, and in the other, a full glass which she downed in a single gulp. She poured herself another and repeated the procedure.

"Would you like to get out of here?" Hope asked. "I could give you a tour of the parsonage."

"I would like that."

Bliss sensed Hope needed a friend at the moment. She didn't know who was guilty of what around here, but lunch had assured her that more than one person in Logan's family was troubled.

"I imagine it takes a while to find your way around this place," Bliss said, following Hope who avoided the living room and her mother-in-law by exiting through the hallway.

"This place is a monstrosity, too big for anyone to actually live in."

"Even with so many family members?"

"There's plenty of room for privacy," Hope admitted. "Even when you don't want it. Let's go upstairs to the third floor. That's where Dean and I live . . . when we have time to be together. Joelle has her suite of rooms there also."

Hope didn't sound thrilled about the latter. She didn't sound enchanted with communal living in general. Bliss had the impression Hope had envisioned a very different sort of life for herself. Bliss didn't think she would like living so close to her husband's family, either, not that that was in the realm of possibilities. She'd never even thought seriously about marriage.

They ascended a polished staircase made of oak inlaid with black walnut and maple, which split the mansion in two. Osmond and his wife undoubtedly had the entire second floor as their private quarters since both their children had moved out. Of course, if the televangelist had his way, Logan would accept the succession and, therefore, move back in. The thought made Bliss unaccountably uneasy, even though it had nothing to do with her. After all, she and Logan weren't right for each other. There was no reason for the thought to bother her.

When they reached the third floor and she saw the size of the private living and sitting rooms added to the countless doorways leading to even more rooms, she realized Hope had a valid point. A person could get lost in the place. The parsonage really was too big for normal living. Osmond must have had grandiose plans for an extended family when he built his home.

"Can I get you something to drink?" Hope asked. "We have a compact kitchen up here, not that we use it much. But I can get you a soft drink or a cup of coffee."

"No thanks. I'm fine. I just came along to be company."

"I appreciate that."

Hope led her into a comfortable-looking room with two separate seating areas, one close to the oversize windows. This room was much less fussy and frilly than any she'd seen downstairs, and yet it was quite femininely decorated in cream and beige with touches of amber and yellow. Floral paintings dominated two walls and crystal vases filled with roses were arranged on the fireplace mantel and on a high, narrow table backing the free-standing couch.

"Sit down," Hope said.

"I've been sitting all morning. My legs could use a little stretching."

"I don't blame you for being nervous after that scene downstairs."

Bliss sensed the strain the episode had caused Hope. Her transformation was disturbing. She seemed brittle almost to the point of snapping. Trying to relieve the tension, Bliss said, "Big families can be difficult."

"Especially this one. Not every family has to deal with an Osmond Wright personality."

"He is bigger than life sometimes." Bliss realized she was mouthing her sister's words, as Melody had described her employer. "But I guess he would have to be to succeed at what he does."

"True, but he doesn't have to run over the members of his own family."

Bliss wandered over to the fireplace and wedged her back against the mantel. "Are you talking about Dean?"

"All of us, but he's especially hard on my husband. I don't understand why Osmond allowed him to become an integral part of the ministry in the first place." Hope fingered the yellow-and-cream challis scarf she wore draped over one shoulder. "He never gives Dean credit for his ideas—when he bothers to listen. He constantly makes him feel as if he's fighting for survival by touting the way Logan will do things when he takes over."

Bliss started. "Wait a minute—I thought Logan didn't want to become a minister."

Hope laughed bitterly. "You don't know The Reverend Wright very well. He usually gets what he wants in the end. Osmond will find a way to control Logan just as he controls my husband."

Bliss crossed to one of the floor-to-ceiling windows so Hope wouldn't see her agitation. "Logan told me the ministry was everything to Dean."

"He's right. And Dean is a really good man who deserves to get everything he's worked all his life for. He deserves more respect from Osmond."

Distracted by her view out the window, Bliss was only half listening. She caught a glimpse of a tall, well-built man with blond hair moving furtively around the far perimeter of the garden. She frowned. The guy looked familiar. She'd seen him before....

"Roger Cahnman?"

She didn't realize she'd verbalized the name until Hope jumped up and rushed across the room.

"What? Where?"

"There, in the garden."

But when Bliss looked down again to point him out, the man was gone.

"There's no one in the garden, now," Hope stated. "Maybe you saw one of the grounds keepers, but certainly not Roger. Osmond fired him some time ago. He'd have no reason to come back."

"Well, just in case," Bliss said, turning from the window, "we should alert Osmond."

Grabbing her by the arm, Hope stopped Bliss from leaving. "No! Roger and Osmond had a fight. A physical altercation. After the fiasco at lunch, Osmond's heart might not take another unpleasant shock."

"Maybe you're right." Bliss's mind was buzzing. She remembered studying the picture in Melody's apartment and wondering if Roger had been the man with whom her sister had fallen in love. "Do you think Roger could have been the man Melody disappeared with?" she asked before realizing she wasn't supposed to know either the former lighting director or her own sister.

Hope gave her a peculiar look. "No, of course not. That's ridiculous."

Maybe. Maybe not. Hope might be right about keeping her supposition from Osmond, but Bliss would tell Logan what she had seen anyway. She checked her watch.

"Time to get back to work. My supervisor will be irritated if I'm late again," Bliss joked.

"Your supervisor is going to be late." Hope was looking at herself in the mirror over the mantel, fussing with her scarf. "I'm not exactly in the mood to rush right back to work. Actually I'll be working in the finance office this afternoon. But we might as well go downstairs and see what's going on.''

Hope led the way. When they arrived at the first floor, everyone seemed to have disappeared. The dining-room table was still laden with half-eaten lunches, however.

"I'll clear the table and see you at the office in a while,'' Hope said, grabbing a couple of plates.

"Are you sure you don't want me to help you?''

"No, of course not.'' Hope's smile seemed forced. "You were supposed to be a guest, after all.''

"See you, then.''

About to leave, Bliss wondered if Logan could still be sequestered with his cousin. She'd noted the room they'd entered off the hall. Probably one of the offices Hope mentioned. Maybe Logan was ready to head back to the studio and they could walk together. If not, she could make an assignation to meet him later. She couldn't wait to tell him about seeing Roger Cahnman, for despite Hope's protest, Bliss was sure he had been in the garden.

The question was, how many other times had the blond man been on the grounds in the past few days?

DEAN SAT IN OSMOND'S OFFICE alone, staring into space. Why did it always have to be like this? Why did he always have to come out of his skirmishes with Osmond feeling like less than a competent man?

A knock at the door startled him. "Come in.''

The panel swung open and Bliss Griffith poked her head in. "Sorry to disturb you, but I'm looking for Logan.''

"He left for the studio a few minutes ago.''

"Sorry—''

"No, don't be. Come in, Bliss, please. I've been wanting to talk to you."

Dean smiled when Bliss entered the room. She was one of the reasons he'd been dragging his heels about bringing up the health spa idea. He'd been too preoccupied with her presence in the ministry to worry about anything else, but his mother hadn't known that when she had forced the issue at lunch, and he wasn't about to explain.

His mother already knew too much.

"What did you want to discuss?" Bliss asked, taking a seat.

"You."

Her tone muted, she said, "I don't understand."

"I have a feeling about you. I think you're exactly what I'm looking for. It would be a sin to confine such an angelic-looking creature as yourself to the ranks of a large choir when you have so much more to offer."

"More?" Her expression was wary. "Like what?"

"I think you could help me guide my spiritual community and enrich its offerings."

Dean forced himself to relax, to submerge himself in the smooth-talking identity he assumed weekly for the benefit of his congregation. He couldn't afford to alarm her if he wanted his plan to work.

"How?"

"The ministry needs an influx of fresh blood and fresh ideas to deal with the modern age. Uncle Osmond is content to leave things the way they've been for decades. That's why he just doesn't appeal to the younger generation."

"But you do."

"I have my own followers, yes, though I would like to see my segment of the congregation multiply. Then I could find the means to back my own ideas."

"I still don't understand what I could do to help."

"I want you to work closely with me. You could appear on the show, both as a soloist and to present some of our products and hype our funding campaigns. You have a certain aura about you that people would trust and respond to. Even if you only took over the responsibility of presenting our Bibles and hymnbooks for which we ask affordable donations, I'm sure our funding program would step up. Then I'd be able to implement a variety of new programs on my own."

"Let me get this straight. You want me to make religious advertisements for you?"

"If you prefer to think of it that way. My intentions are exemplary," Dean assured her. "I've found a disturbing trend toward lack of spirituality in our young people today. I want to bring them back to God's house using whatever methods I must."

"That's a tall order."

"One that I'm ready to fill. What do you say? Are you with me? Will you help me bring God's children back to him?"

Though she seemed flattered, Bliss said, "I hadn't thought of playing such an important role in the ministry. I would like to think about this."

"Fair enough. You'll practice with the Singing Angels tomorrow. Rehearsal ends about an hour before my show is broadcast. If you wait on stage, I'll join you there before going back to my dressing room for makeup. You can give me your answer then."

"Fine."

Exultant, Dean rose and escorted her to the door. Things were starting to fall into place. This plan would work. It had to. He was running out of ideas.

LOGAN TRADED THE BUSY HUB of master control, with its hum of electronic equipment and music and voices coming from various speakers, for the relative peace and quiet of his office. He needed some time alone to think. Everything seemed to be crashing in on him at once and he paced his office like a caged animal.

A woman he considered his friend had disappeared, his father had been threatened, both Bliss and he had barely escaped attacks on their lives, and now the members of his family were at one another's throats—and there wasn't a thing he could do about any of it.

One thing, perhaps. He just couldn't bring himself to sacrifice his entire life to serve others. He thought of himself as a good person, but his liberal attitudes would make him a rotten minister. Besides, what would acceding to his father's desires accomplish other than to slow Osmond down a bit and to cause an even wider rift between Dean and himself.

Logan wished he had a punching bag so he could let off some steam. He guessed he could punch the wall, but the way his luck was going, he would break his hand.

He and Dean had been as close as brothers once, but now his cousin seemed almost like a stranger to him. Although they had talked for a good while in his father's office, Logan had sensed his cousin's deep-seated antagonism even while Dean tried to be openly appreciative of his support. The other man just couldn't help resenting him.

A knock at the door interrupted his disturbing thoughts. "Entrance by invitation only," he shouted, as he always did when he was too busy to be disturbed. But this visitor ignored him and entered anyway, almost whacking him in the face with the door. "Bliss."

"Can we have a few minutes alone?"

"After I close this. In your hands, a door could be a lethal weapon."

He did so, then stood close enough to her that he was tempted to take her into his arms. That was one way to forget his problems for the moment, not that she would approve. Still, he felt as if an influence that was at once calming and stimulating had swept into his office like a warm Caribbean breeze. A small hurricane, he silently corrected with a smile. Even so, her mere presence made him feel better already. He couldn't resist picking up a lock of her hair and winding the golden strands around a finger.

"Now what did you have in mind?" he asked, arching an eyebrow.

"Wipe that silly grin off your face," she ordered softly.

He could tell she was fighting their mutual attraction, as usual. What flowed between them was becoming more than an attraction for him and that was something he didn't want to think about, so he covered by teasing her.

"Don't you like my smile?"

"I didn't say that. But I'm beginning to think I can read your mind and what's up there isn't appropriate for in here."

"The black sheep strikes again, huh?" he teased.

"Strikes out, you mean."

"Ouch. My ego."

"Get a grip on it. I saw Roger Cahnman on the grounds earlier."

Immediately straightening, Logan let go of her hair. "Roger—where?"

"In the garden. While you went to console your cousin, Hope wanted some company so I went upstairs with her. I was looking out the window when I spotted him."

"Are you sure it was Roger?"

"As sure as I can be without ever having met the man. I suppose he could be a grounds keeper like Hope said, but I've never seen this guy around before. I swear he was the same Roger Cahnman that you identified in Melody's picture."

"Hope was with you. Did she see him?"

"No. I forgot myself and his name came flying out of my mouth," Bliss said in disgust. "Not that Hope seemed to notice. She came running over to the window, but by the time she got there, the man had disappeared from view. She said she didn't believe Roger would come back after the fight he'd had with your father. I wanted to warn Osmond in case I was right, but Hope stopped me. She said your father's heart couldn't take the added strain after the episode at lunch."

"How nice of her to be so concerned about Father for once."

"She did give me the feeling that she and Osmond aren't the best of friends."

"They never have been." Logan thought about the way his father tried to run other people's lives. "He didn't really approve of Dean's choice for a wife, but for once my cousin did as he wanted by marrying Hope. She would have been good for him if only Dean hadn't continued to put his obsession for my father's approval first."

"Whatever—they aren't under discussion here. Your former lighting director is. What do you think?" Bliss demanded. "Could he be connected to Melody?"

"I don't know, but it looks as if we ought to find out."

"How?"

"We can ask around Wrightville. Damn!" The word exploded off his lips before Logan could suppress it. "I have a broadcast tonight, so our investigation will have to wait until tomorrow. I'll think of some excuse to leave early so all the shops will still be open when we get to town."

"Do you really think we'll find out anything?"

"Wrightville is a small town. If Roger has been around, more than one person is bound to have seen him."

And if they tracked down the former lighting director and learned the man was the one responsible for all the problems at the ministry—Logan might be tempted to use him as a human punching bag.

THE WOMAN DROVE her car along the gravel road to the meeting place in the heart of the Hoosier National Forest. The mounting stress of the past few days combined with anticipation made her foot press the accelerator a fraction too hard. The spinning wheels raised clouds of dust that billowed behind her. They needed rain badly, but she no longer cared if the Midwest had another drought.

For once in her life, she was thinking only about herself, about the myriad delights that would be her compensation for all she had endured. Some pleasures she would take now, others would come later. But she had already waited long enough for her due, hadn't she?

She deserved to reap the rewards of the plan she had masterminded.

The road curved to the right. A moment later, she swung the car to the left onto a narrow dirt track that wound through a thick stand of dogwood and black walnut trees, and down a gentle slope to a small clearing fringed by white pine. The place was perfect, invisible from the main road and vice versa.

But he knew she was coming.

The screen door creaked open just as she braked and fled the vehicle. He waited for her, his eyes hooded, expression masked, stance rigid—the epitome of male indifference.

She could easily change that attitude. Funny how naturally power had come to her once she had decided to take it. Her heart beat faster as she thought about what he would give her. She had a bone to pick with him, but complaints could wait until later. Both of their moods would be better then, and she would handle him more easily.

She slid into his arms and noted that he didn't instantly accommodate her. His shoulder was still stiff from the wound, she told herself. That was all.

"It's been too long," she murmured.

"I agree. When are we going to pull this off?"

It irritated her that he was talking about the scheme while she was interested in a more intimate conversation. Pressing herself against him, she felt his response despite his mental resistance.

"When I say," she murmured into his ear before nibbling the lobe. His indrawn breath made her smile. "Soon." She gently bit the juncture between his neck and shoulder and felt the hard flesh quiver. "A matter of a few more days." Her tongue laved the length of his throat. "I don't have all day. We have better things to do than talk right now."

As if to prove her right once more, he swept her off her feet and carried her inside.

BLISS REMAINED PREOCCUPIED as she worked throughout the afternoon. The thing uppermost on her mind was her conversation with Dean, something she hadn't discussed with Logan.

While he had spoken of spirituality, Bliss had heard imaginary cash registers. And yet she was half-convinced that Dean was sincere in his desire to reach potential members of his congregation. If he could move someone who had as much reason to be skeptical as she did, he had inherited his uncle's gift of persuasion. And if a hearty dose of self-confidence was added to his persona, Dean Mackey could be another Osmond Wright someday.

A notion startled her so much that she dropped an entire stack of flyers on the floor: could Melody have fallen for Dean?

Good grief. The only man she hadn't mentally paired her sister with was Gregory Townsend. Though she'd immediately added together the phone call and the altered books as reason to suspect the man, she had since discarded the idea. The financial director would have cleverly hidden his dishonesty. Besides, a man with his income potential would have gone for the big bucks. Someone else, someone who occasionally filled in at the finance office was undoubtedly to blame for the discrepancies.

She was on her knees, taking care of the mess when the office door opened and heels clacked across the tiled floor, stopping in front of her. Bliss rose, arms full, to meet a pair of penetrating blue eyes.

"Lurlene. Can I help you?"

"I was on my way back to the parsonage and I wondered if you would like to accompany me."

"Uhh, sure…if you can give me a minute to straighten up this mess."

"I'll wait."

Making quick work of the job, she tried to smother her involuntary wariness. It was no use. Everyone in the ministry was suspect. Logan's mother hadn't just happened to be in the office. She'd stopped by purposely.

Bliss couldn't help but wonder what in the world Lurlene Wright wanted with her.

# Chapter Ten

"I wanted to apologize for lunch," Lurlene told Bliss as they set off across the grounds together. "I'm sure our little family squabble made you uncomfortable."

"All families have arguments."

"Yes, but not usually in front of a guest, especially not one who is a mere acquaintance of a few family members."

*Of Logan.* Bliss could almost hear his mother think the name, and she felt Lurlene's eyes slide to her for a reaction. She kept her expression pleasantly bland. So they were about to get right to the heart of the matter. Maybe this would give her a chance to do a little investigating in return.

"Don't worry, I wasn't shocked or offended." Bliss watched her step as they descended the hill even though they had taken the paved path. As usual, she was wearing heels and a dress and, therefore, was wary of the steep decline. "And I won't go spreading tales around the ministry."

"I wasn't afraid that you would." Lurlene hesitated only a heartbeat before adding, "What...rather *who* I am worried about is my son."

So she'd been right. Bliss asked, "Why? Is he ill or in trouble."

"More like troubled, as in distressed. My intuition tells me something's bothering Logan. I thought he might have confided in you."

Bliss could have sworn there was a false note in her speech, but she couldn't pinpoint what—or her reason for thinking so. She decided to remain noncommittal. "As you said, we're only acquaintances."

"Sometimes a person confides more about his troubles to an acquaintance than to those who are really close to him."

"I know that Logan is worried about his father." Now it was Bliss's turn to give Lurlene a sly glance. "And about Osmond's insistence on his taking a more aggressive role in the ministry."

"Yes, his father can be quite stubborn on that particular issue," she admitted. "While I don't blame Logan for wanting to visit with his father more frequently after Osmond's surgery, and while I love having my son around, he should have stayed where he was and concentrated on his chosen career."

"You don't approve of your husband's desire to have his own son succeed him?"

This pause was longer and definitely indicated Lurlene was uncomfortable. But Bliss had to give the older woman credit. Logan's mother schooled her features into a passive mask and was able to control her speech with equal effectiveness.

"I want my son to be happy. He has neither the calling nor the temperament to be a minister. To tell you the truth, I was happy for him when he wanted to go out on his own. Heading a ministry is an all-consuming passion. It doesn't leave time for much else."

Bliss noted the sadness in her voice and wondered who it was for—Logan or herself.

"Hope said much the same thing."

"Poor child. She married Dean with such high expectations. I'm afraid she's been disillusioned."

Just as Lurlene had been? Bliss wondered. "By what? The work or the life-style?"

"Neither. I think she could have handled both. But it's not Hope that I'm concerned about." As they approached the parsonage, Lurlene deftly changed the subject. "I was going to cut some flowers for the dinner table. Would you like to join me in the garden? I'll cut some for you as well."

Unable to resist getting a closer look at the area where she'd seen Roger Cahnman without arousing suspicions, Bliss agreed. "That would be lovely."

She followed Logan's mother around the back to the garden. From a supply shed, Lurlene took two handled baskets, a pair of leather gloves and pruning shears. Even while appreciating the beauty of the spring blooms, some of which were already giving way to the greenery of summer, Bliss looked for signs of the man she'd seen. Not that she had any idea what she might find helpful. A couple of large footprints in the soft earth could not be classified as a clue, however, and so she soon gave up the useless task.

She turned back to Logan's mother who was already filling the baskets with late-blooming tulips, grape hyacinths and Dutch iris.

"Gardening is such a soothing task," Lurlene told her, adding a couple of lilies to the bouquets. "It can be a wonderful therapy during the milder half of the year. These bulbs will give way to summer perennials and then to fall mums. Working with indoor plants in the winter is not nearly as satisfying.''

Wondering why she had suddenly turned off the inquisition and was trying to make small talk, Bliss said, ''Hope told me she enjoyed gardening, too.''

''Yes. We don't often work together, however.''

''Lurlene, why don't you be straight with me.'' Bliss crossed her arms and stood over the woman who knelt directly in the rich black earth. ''You didn't stop by the office on a whim. What is it you really want to know?''

Placing the pruning shears in one of the baskets, she stood and dusted off her skirt. ''All right, then. I want to know if my son means anything to you.''

''I like him, of course. Logan can be charming.'' When he wanted to be.

''You like him. No more?''

A lot more, but she needn't share that information with the older woman. ''I've known him less than a week.''

''Love doesn't always take its time.'' Lurlene picked up both baskets and stared down at her precious flowers. ''It can sneak up on you in a matter of minutes.''

Bliss felt her neck redden. ''I guess so.''

''I can tell you don't want to answer me directly. But if you do love Logan, let him know it.'' She looked at Bliss seriously. ''Then get him out of here before it's too late.''

Lurlene handed her one of the baskets, then rushed off, and before Bliss could respond, entered a door at the back of the house. Amazed, she stood speechless and staring.

What had that been about?

Did the woman know anything about the danger she and Logan were in?

Bliss hadn't forgotten the gray bond stationery that Erma had said the office-supply store stocked mainly for Lurlene Wright. She had entertained the notion that Osmond's wife might be sending him threatening notes but had just as quickly dismissed the suspicion.

But maybe too quickly?

While Lurlene hadn't made any specific statements about being dissatisfied with her own lot, she had voiced her gratitude that Logan had chosen another life . . . and she'd expressed her pity for Hope who had been disillusioned by hers. Then she'd given that baffling warning.

How could she connect Lurlene's statement with threats and violence? With a shiver, Bliss started toward the apartment complex. An unpaved path through the rose garden seemed to be the most direct route. Holding the basket in one hand, her skirts with the other so they wouldn't get caught by sharp thorns, she set off, her mind dwelling on the puzzle pieces that still did not make a whole.

Lurlene might be capable of making a threat, but she couldn't possibly have been responsible for the violence. Bliss had no trouble recognizing a man's strength and voice.

A sudden thought made her stop dead in her tracks in the middle of the rosebushes.

*There had to be two of them working together!*

That's why there seemed to be so many arrows pointing in different directions. Now all she and Logan had to do was figure out which were the right arrows to follow. They had to decide what might link two people together in a common cause. Then maybe they would be able to fit the pieces together and come up with some answers.

THE NEXT MISSIVE WAS READY for delivery. The author reread it one last time.

To Osmond Wright—
  Ecclesiastes 12.14. *For God shall bring every work into judgment, with every secret thing, whether it be good, or whether it be evil.*
  Your secrets are no longer safe, Osmond. His judgment is nearer than you think and I have appointed myself His executioner here on earth. Be prepared to pay or forfeit all.

One who knows

With gloved hands the author folded the note and slipped it into an envelope.

If only Bliss and Logan would pay attention to warnings as Osmond would have to.

The two of them kept poking their noses where they didn't belong and were proving to be quite annoying. Melody's sister should have stayed where she belonged. Then neither she nor Logan would ever have been hurt.

And the plan wouldn't have to be speeded up.

Osmond would have no choice but to pay attention to *this* warning unless he wanted to find himself scrounging for a living on some back street in Louisville. How ironic if he were forced to return to his roots. The blackmailer had no compunctions about what they were doing to him, no regrets about what might happen to the televangelist.

Stripping Reverend Osmond Wright of everything he held dear would be nothing more than serving him his just deserts.

"THE FIRST THING WE CAN DO is check with the post office to see if Roger Cahnman left a forwarding address," Logan said, heading his red Fiero for Wrightville the next afternoon.

"A postal clerk would just give it to us for the asking?"

"For a modest fee. One of our helpful governmental services."

Going to the post office reminded Bliss of the last time she'd been there. She could almost see the letter addressed to a Louisville box number in flowing handwriting. She still hadn't told Logan about the stationery.

On impulse, she asked, "Does your mother have some reason she wants to be rid of you?"

Bliss was surprised when the question didn't shock Logan. He merely gave her an inquisitive glance before turning his attention back to the road.

"Not that I know of. Why?"

"She told me that if I cared about you, I should tell you so and—"

"Do you?" he interrupted, looking at her with more interest this time. He clasped her hand and wouldn't allow her to withdraw it.

"She said I should tell you so," Bliss patiently repeated, determined that he would not get her off the track. "And get you away from here before it's too late."

That sobered him. "Too late? When was this?"

Bliss explained the circumstances leading up to Lurlene's warning.

"Missing funds...threats...missing Melody," Logan chanted. "Sounds like a litany. If only we could connect it all somehow."

"I've been thinking about that. We know a man is involved for sure. Let's assume that person is Roger Cahnman. He couldn't be doing everything alone because he's no longer working for the ministry. Someone inside is tracking our movements...therefore, that person probably sent your father the threat."

"Like who?" Logan's voice went flat and he let go of her hand. "My mother?"

"Could be."

"What?" he shouted, turning stormy gray eyes on her. "Because of some vague warning she made?"

"Don't get excited and keep your eyes on the road."

Bliss reached over and turned his face toward the windshield. In doing so, she got a closer look at Logan's bruised temple peeking out from behind a fringe of curls. At least her throat didn't have to be hidden under collars or scarves any longer. She merely had to apply makeup to cover the fading bruises.

"Just hear me out," she continued. "Lurlene gave me the feeling she wasn't too happy with her life. Maybe she just wants out."

"So she sends threats to my father instead of asking for a divorce?"

"I didn't say anything about a divorce. Maybe she wants to keep him...but not the ministry. If he started getting threats, she could use them to convince him to retire."

"And then she hires Roger Cahnman to do away with you, not to mention her only son."

"All right. That doesn't make sense," Bliss admitted. "Maybe we have more than one thing going on here."

"You're grasping at straws."

"Remember the threat was typed on gray bond," she said, finally getting to the point. "Your mother uses the same stationery. Erma looked for some at the office-supply store and they told her Lurlene had bought the last box.''

"I know about the stationery. My mother was working on some correspondence when I went to see her the other night and I recognized the paper on her desk."

"And you didn't say anything?"

"Well, you didn't say anything, either, did you?" Logan's tone was appropriately caustic. "Anyone in the household has access to Mother's office and could take a few sheets of paper and matching envelopes without her ever missing them."

Setting her jaw, Bliss slid closer to the door and stared out at the houses at the edge of town. "I knew this would happen."

"What?"

"That you would try to protect your family at all costs. You must have been thrilled to know I saw your former lighting director. You can pin the blame on him and you won't have to worry about your family."

She tried to ignore the hurt she was feeling because it said too much about her growing feelings for Logan.

"Being able to prove Roger is the only guilty one would be the best-case scenario, but whether or not you believe me, Bliss, I want to learn the truth whatever it is. Your sister may be a victim of a crime, but so is my father."

"Let's stop right there." She couldn't help herself; she had to make him face an uncomfortable truth. "If Osmond is so innocent, then why did he receive that threat? Why did the note say he should look to his own sins? The sender knows something your father wants kept secret."

Logan swept right over her last statement. "I don't for a moment believe my mother is involved. She may have occasional complaints about her situation as everyone does, but she loves my father and would protect him from harm, no matter what she had to do."

His statement opened another possibility for Bliss, although she dared not verbalize it. Would Lurlene get rid of someone she thought of as competition, someone who could come between her and her husband?

Back to Melody and Osmond again. The problem was that no matter how hard she tried, Bliss couldn't make the picture stick. She just didn't believe that they had been lovers.

Logan turned the Fiero onto Main Street and parked in front of the post office. When they entered, an uneasy silence lay between them. Luckily the place was empty except for the gray-haired man behind the counter. He was the same postal clerk who'd been there when she'd helped Joelle with the mail the day before.

"John, how are you doing?" Logan asked.

"Not so bad now that the weather's warming up."

"Arthritis getting to you?"

"Every time it gets damp. But I'll be retiring this year. Becky and me are moving to Phoenix before winter sets in."

"We'll all miss you."

"I'll miss everyone around here, but not the snow, I can tell you that," John said, giving Bliss a curious look. "So, Logan, what can I do for you today?"

"I was wondering if you could give me a new address for Roger Cahnman. He left the ministry a month or so ago and moved out of the apartment complex, but he forgot to take a few personal things," Logan explained. "I thought I would send them to him."

John shrugged. "Nice idea . . . if the fella ever decides to give us a change of address."

Bliss felt new excitement stir her adrenaline. No change of address. That meant Cahnman didn't want to be found. He might, indeed, still be around.

"Maybe you should check your files," Logan suggested.

"My body might be getting old, but my mind is as sharp as ever. I've got mail waiting for him in back, not that he gets much. All that will have to go into the dead file pretty soon."

"I could take it off your hands—"

"Tch-tch. You should know better than that, Logan. I can't turn someone else's mail over to you. It wouldn't be legal."

"Right, John. Sorry. I wouldn't want to get you into any trouble. Well, if you hear from Cahnman, give me a call, would you?"

"I'll surely do that."

Back out on the street a moment later, Bliss shook her head. "Lying to the man, then trying to get him to do something illegal. I don't know about you, Logan Wright."

"Resourcefulness is only one of my many creative attributes. Stick around. You'll learn about the others quickly enough."

A comfortable warmth flowed through Bliss as she realized his earlier anger with her had dissipated. "You have other vices you'd care to tell me about?"

"I'm not even going to touch that one. Let's get busy and find out if our man found another residence in the area."

They spent the next hour combing every store on Main Street, describing Roger Cahnman to those shopkeepers who didn't know him, and asking if anyone had seen the blond man around during the past few weeks. They got a few maybes, but nothing positive.

Discouraged, Bliss said, "Well, this is getting us nowhere fast."

"Hmm. I have an idea." Logan placed a hand in the middle of Bliss's back and steered her in the direction from which they'd come. "We're going to pay a visit to a nice lady named Mrs. Donnelly."

"Older woman in a white elephant of a house with a swing on the front porch?"

"You met her?"

"Not exactly. Joelle shouted a greeting to the woman from the car yesterday," she said. She recalled Logan's aunt saying the ministry family was the closest thing to royalty the town had. "What makes you think she would know about Cahnman?"

"Mrs. Donnelly sees everyone who comes and goes through town past her place. In good weather, she sits in her porch swing practically from dawn to dusk. When it gets too cold, she sits in front of her picture window instead."

"Some people have odd ideas about entertainment."

"She calls herself a student of humanity."

Bliss had to laugh. A more apt description might be town busybody. But a short while later when they met, she was glad for the woman's predilection for keeping an eye on the town's goings-on. Logan's inquiry drew an immediate positive response from Mrs. Donnelly.

"Yes, I know the man you mean."

The elderly woman looked up from Logan to Bliss with a speculative gleam in her sharp brown eyes. How long would it take her to spread rumors of a budding romance? Bliss wondered.

"Drives a tan Plymouth Voyager, right?" Mrs. Donnelly was asking.

"That's him," Logan acceded.

"He's been around a couple of times since your daddy fired him from the ministry. Gets groceries and gas across the way at the general store."

"Are you positive?" Bliss asked. "We checked there, but no one could tell us for sure that Cahnman has been around."

Mrs. Donnelly looked up over the tip of her long nose at Bliss. "Young people don't have as much time to notice details as we old folks do. When you don't have a lot of other things crowding your mind, you concentrate on what goes on around you. Yes, young lady, I am positive that I have seen the man Logan described."

"I didn't mean any offense."

"None taken."

Logan intervened smoothly. "When was the last time you saw Roger?"

"Why, yesterday. He filled up his tank right after this young lady and your aunt stopped for gas and groceries. He comes past here off of Harmony Road and goes back the same way," the elderly woman continued. "Must be living someplace north of here in the woods."

Logan gave Bliss a look of triumph. "Thank you, Mrs. Donnelly. You've been a great help."

Bliss put her hand on Logan's arm to stop him from leaving as he was about to do. "One more thing, Mrs. Donnelly. Do you remember seeing a black Lincoln pull into the store's lot yesterday?"

"I remember."

"Have you ever seen that car around here before?"

"Yep. A few days ago. I'm afraid I can't remember exactly when, though."

Bliss forced a smile to her lips. "Thank you."

As they walked to the car, Logan asked, "What was that all about?"

"Arden Heath. In addition to him being here yesterday, he was also in town a few days ago. I was attacked on Monday and you were attacked on Wednesday. For all we know, he might have been conveniently around both times."

"You're complicating things again."

Knowing Logan hadn't liked her theory about Heath blackmailing his father, Bliss didn't say another word. He opened the car door for her and she slid into her seat.

Maybe she *was* complicating things . . . and maybe Logan wouldn't be willing to believe the truth even if it hit him square in the nose.

LOGAN TRIED not to let himself get aggravated again as he pulled the car onto Harmony Road. "This leads into the Hoosier National Forest. My cabin isn't far away."

"Is that where you're taking me?"

"Is that where you want to go?" When she didn't answer, he said, "There aren't too many people living out this way. I thought we could look for a tan Voyager."

A few minutes later, Harmony split off from a larger road that led to other towns, and they headed past a couple of working farms toward the forest itself. He slowed and shifted into a lower gear as pavement turned to gravel. Even with rubber mud flaps, his paint job suffered from the pings made by stones bouncing off the car's surface every time he headed for or left his place. Then again, he hadn't known he would be living in rural Indiana when he'd bought the sports car.

They spent the next half hour combing the driveways and dirt tracks off the gravel road that led to houses, and more frequently, trailer homes. They found cars and trucks and even horses, but no Voyager.

And all the while, Logan's concentration was split between thoughts of his prey and the silent woman beside him. Why did Bliss have to be so impossible? Were her preconceived ideas about televangelists so set that she refused to believe his father could be as honest and as moral as any man? It was as if she were determined to pin something on him. And his mother, for that matter.

It was just his luck to have fallen for the wrong sister. With her sweetness and sincere religious convictions, Melody would have made him a far more suitable mate. But then he had never fallen in love with her.

That he was thinking in terms of commitment jarred him, made him grit his teeth, but he couldn't rid himself of the notion: he had fallen head over heels for a stubborn, feisty, opinionated, angelic-looking woman.

Simply put, he was in love with Bliss.

Frustrated by this irrefutable fact, Logan shifted to a higher gear, stepped on the gas and left a spray of gravel behind them. How could this have happened when they hadn't even gone on a single date? All they seemed to do was fight. And Bliss kept reminding him that they were wrong for each other.

He was so distracted by such thoughts that, halfway back to Wrightville, when a tan Voyager nosed its way out of a stand of dogwood and black walnut trees, he almost missed it, until Bliss snapped him out of his trancelike state.

"Logan, look!"

Following her pointing finger to the driveway he'd used many times, Logan let up on the accelerator in surprise. What the hell was Roger doing there? Had someone let him stay on the property? Or had he broken in, figuring no one would find him right under their noses?

"What are you waiting for? Step on it—that's him!" Bliss cried as the other vehicle swung wide in front of them.

Logan didn't have time to explain things to her as Roger seemed to realize who was behind him. Then the Voyager took off like a shot, spewing a trail of gravel at them. Logan made sure the Fiero stayed on its tail, just out of reach of the rocky missiles.

"Now that we've found him, how are we going to make him stop?" Bliss asked.

"One thing at a time. I have to keep up with him first."

"Are you kidding? In this car?"

"If we were on the highway, he wouldn't have a chance of getting away from us. But gravel roads weren't made for sports cars."

"He'll have to get off the gravel sometime."

"That's what I'm afraid of."

Their quarry did just that, swinging the Voyager onto a rutted dirt track that cut across someone's farm. Logan followed, though his hopes for keeping up with the other vehicle were faltering. Clenching his jaw against the bumps, he hoped the constant jarring wouldn't make his head start aching. He did his best to keep up, even taking the Fiero through a meadow where cows grazed. But when Roger kept going through a newly sprouting field of corn that was being irrigated, Logan stepped on the brake and hit the steering wheel with the flat of his hand.

"Damn!"

"Aren't you even going to try to go after him?"

"Through those mud flats? We'll be stuck before we get halfway across. Then you would have to get out in your high heels and push."

"And probably lose both shoes, this time." Bliss clenched her fists as the other vehicle disappeared from sight. "I've never been so frustrated."

Wondering which of them felt more let down, Logan attempted to relieve their tension by injecting some humor into the situation. "I could do something about your frustration if you really wanted me to."

"What is that supposed to mean?" she asked suspiciously.

With her hair tangled around her face and shoulders and her skin flushed with color from the wind, Bliss looked gorgeous. His attempt at a joke suddenly turned serious.

"I could show you."

Logan slid one leg over the stick shift so that he was practically sharing her bucket seat. Before she could voice the objection that he was certain was coming, he wrapped his arms around her. She might be able to lie to herself about what might be between them, but she couldn't lie to him.

"You really are beautiful when you're arguing with me."

Bliss pushed his chest for release, but he refused to give over.

"Logan, this is neither the time nor the place—"

"It never is for you."

"Will you think with your brain instead of your hormones."

"Hormones, huh? Do you really have yourself convinced that physical attraction is the only thing we have going between us?"

"Yes."

"Liar," he said softly. He knew he was correct when alarm shadowed her eyes.

"Right now we should be going back to that road where Roger came out of the woods and see what's there. Do you think you could get your wits about you long enough to find the road again?"

"Oh, yes, I'm positive I could find it. Promise me something first," Logan insisted, not liking the obstinate expression on her face. "Don't scowl at me like that. I'm not going to ask for your firstborn child." At least not yet. Probably never, he thought regretfully. "All I want is some time alone with you tonight. Dinner at my place."

"To discuss our clues?"

"Anything but. We're both stressed out. We need to relax."

"I, uh, can't."

"You mean you don't want to."

"I have a rehearsal from seven to eight, and then I promised Dean I would stay to talk to him before he got ready for his broadcast."

"Dean? What does he want?"

"Something about making me part of *his* ministry. An attempt at competing with your father, I guess."

"I have to be around for his broadcast anyway, remember? But I like late dinners." With one hand free, Logan ran a finger along her jawline. "They're romantic."

"That's what I'm afraid of."

"Are you afraid of me?"

"No." Bliss glared at him as she corrected herself. "Yes."

"Good. That makes us even. Promise and we can go."

She didn't answer immediately, and he wondered what scheme was running through her mind. Her answer surprised him.

"All right. I promise. But I'm taking my car," she added quickly.

"Any way I can get you there," Logan muttered, already sliding back into place behind the wheel.

He was probably crazy, asking for trouble, but he felt a sense of triumph that he couldn't minimize. He drove back off the farmer's property a happy man.

Five minutes later, they were on the gravel road, approaching the dirt track that disappeared into the stand of trees.

"That's the road Roger came from, isn't it?" Bliss asked.

"Right."

What truths might he learn at the bottom of the hill? Logan wondered. He swung the Fiero onto the road and took it easy over the ruts. He could feel renewed tension building inside.

"Look," she said, pointing to the clearing ahead. "A trailer. Do you think Roger has been staying there? If so, maybe something inside will lead us to my sister."

Logan pulled the car in front of the place. "Maybe. This is really puzzling, but—"

Before he could explain where they were, Bliss vaulted out of the passenger seat and sprinted across the grass. She banged at the trailer's door.

"Anyone in there? Hello?"

He was hardly out of the car and she was already trying to get in. She opened the trailer door.

"Wait a minute," he called. "It might not be safe!"

But she was already inside.

Logan jogged over to the trailer and followed her inside just as she reentered the main room from the back bedroom.

"Find anything?" he asked.

Bliss shook her head. "Not exactly. There are some clothes...a few women's things. Either Roger's been staying here with a woman or we're trespassing on some stranger's property."

"I don't think we have to worry about that. I was trying to tell you this trailer and the property it sits on belong to Dean and Hope."

## Chapter Eleven

As they drove back toward town, Bliss tried to keep up her spirits. She was disappointed that they hadn't found some clue in the trailer that would lead them to her sister. Now she had to start over, wonder if Melody was alive or if her faith was nothing more than heartfelt fantasy.... Despair gripped her and for once, she couldn't seem to shake off the chill that seeped into her bones.

"I wonder if Roger was staying at the trailer," Logan said.

"Who would have let him do so?"

"Everyone in the family has access to the place. Then again, Roger might just have been there on his own."

"There were no signs of a break-in," she reminded him. "And we didn't find anything inside to prove he'd been staying there. He merely could have been looking for something."

"True, but someone recently spent time in the trailer. Maybe Hope and Dean."

Bliss made an impatient noise. "Not together."

"Why not?"

"Can you honestly say Dean puts himself out for the wife he defied your father to marry?"

"Not since I returned to this area to live, he hasn't. I don't know about the two previous years."

Hearing guilt in his voice, Bliss said, "It's not your fault that your father is so mule headed."

"But if I had stayed away, things might be different between Father and Dean and, therefore, different between my cousin and his wife."

Bliss was beginning to like Osmond less and less. He might be a good man, an honest minister, but from everything she'd heard about him, he was also a dictator.

"Dean bought that place when they were first married," Logan told her. "They were going to build their own home on that land someday."

"Were. One of nature's little ironies. Dean wouldn't come through with his promise to his wife and live away from your father. Maybe one of them was using it for a tryst."

"You can't be serious."

"Why not? I can draw some conclusions from my observations." Bliss was growing testy. "There were signs of both a man and a woman using that trailer. Men's toiletries in the bathroom, fresh lipstick on a glass in the kitchen sink."

"Are you saying Hope was having an affair?"

Logan slowed the car as they entered the town limits. He was quiet and thoughtful until they made the turnoff toward the ministry compound.

"I didn't say who. Why not Dean? At least Hope still has feelings for her husband. I'm not so certain those feelings are returned. Dean is too busy trying to impress your father to make his own wife happy. That doesn't say much for the effort he has put into the marriage. And who knows? Maybe it's neither of them. Like you said, everyone in the family has access to the place."

They approached the ministry grounds in silence. Logan waved to the security guard at his post as they cruised past the front gates. Bliss checked her watch. She barely had time to shower and change into the one dress she hadn't yet worn. She'd never expected to be gone so long from Indianapolis.

The reminder that she hadn't come any closer to solving the mystery of Melody's disappearance dropped her spirits to a new low. She wasn't in the mood to go to rehearsal, let alone to Logan's place for a late-night dinner.

As if he could read her thoughts, he said, "Tonight will be good for both of us."

"I don't know—"

"Don't try to cop out on me now." He swung the Fiero into the apartment building parking lot and put the car into neutral. "You made a promise."

"Under duress."

"But we both need time out." Logan was at his most convincing when he said, "Maybe for one evening we can forget that both of our worlds have been turned upside down. We can concentrate on us."

If anyone could take her mind off her sister, Bliss knew Logan was that person. "You can be very persuasive."

"Then you won't back out on me?"

He didn't have to know she'd been thinking about doing just that. "I always keep my promises," she replied.

"I'll pick you up in the studio after rehearsal."

"But Dean's show—"

"Yes, I have to be there. You can keep me company and watch the behind-the-scenes magic."

"I could use a little magic right about now."

"Then I'll be happy to provide it."

When he moved closer and his arms reached across her body, Bliss thought he was going to kiss her again. Despite the letdowns of the day, her pulse surged and she suddenly had trouble breathing properly. But the sharp sound of the latch quashed her physical reactions to his closeness.

Logan was only opening the door for her.

"Tonight," he added belatedly, a devilish look in his eyes. "See you later."

His breath teased her cheek as he slowly straightened away from her. Feeling silly, let down and thoroughly confused, Bliss quickly escaped from the car. Logan grinned at her as he made a tight U-turn and pulled out of the lot. And whether she wanted to admit it or not, a tiny piece of her went with him.

Bliss felt choked by what she was feeling for the man, but she couldn't deny it.

She just refused to name the emotion.

BY THE TIME REHEARSAL ENDED less than two hours later, Bliss was feeling much better. Immersing herself in the music had made her forget everything else for a while. Her mood was tranquil and she meant to keep it that way. Perhaps she and Logan really could spend a peaceful evening together.

"I'd like a word with you," Paul Nardini told her as the choir members scattered. "Do you feel ready to debut with the Singing Angels during tomorrow night's broadcast?"

"If you don't think I'll embarrass you."

"I think you'll do us both proud."

"Well, I'll do my best, anyway."

"Good. Erma will be included also, so you won't have to feel alone," the choir director assured her. "*An Hour with Osmond Wright* begins promptly at eight. That means you get to the dressing room at seven. But first you'll have to stop by sometime in the afternoon, let's say three o'clock, so the seamstress can alter one of the choir robes for you. Very few of our Angels have been quite so petite."

Somehow that didn't surprise her. "I'll be here."

Nardini gave her the thumbs-up sign before taking off. Bliss was looking around the almost empty studio for some sign of Dean when she noticed Erma Dixon wave at her. She responded and the woman broke off from a small group that had congregated in the audience.

"Hey, Bliss." Erma stalked her purposefully as the other women ambled toward the exit. "How would you like to join a couple of us on a calorie binge at the ice-cream shop?"

"I can't. I have plans."

"A date?"

"Sort of."

"Uh-uh." Erma pulled a face and shook her head. "Either it *is* a date, or it isn't. No in-betweens."

"Is. I guess."

The studio was empty except for the two of them. Had Dean forgotten about their appointment? Bliss checked her watch. Five past eight. He'd better get there soon. She wasn't sure what time the doors would open to the audience, but she could hear the murmur of voices out in the lobby. The crew members would be out on the floor any minute now. She could hear one of them making a soft scuffling noise behind the set. When she looked over to the flats that would back the choir, she caught a brief glimpse of a shadow behind the stained-glass windows.

"So that's how it is," Erma said, grinning at Bliss.

"Uh, how?"

"You like this guy more than you want to because you're afraid the relationship won't work out."

Bliss was completely serious when she asked, "Are you psychic?"

"Nope. Just a good guesser with lots of experience. I noticed you were looking around for him. I assume the man works here."

"He does, but I wasn't looking for him. I was actually hoping to see Dean Mackey."

Another noise backstage distracted Bliss. She wanted to get this over with because she was becoming impatient. So where was he? It would only take a moment to thank him for his offer and say no thanks. She wasn't willing to get in any further with this member-of-the-flock business than she already was. She wasn't even sure how long she could keep up her present charade.

Realizing Erma was staring at her, Bliss figured she'd aroused the other woman's curiosity. "I don't want to keep you." She added, "Your friends have already left," as a metallic-sounding creak overhead startled her.

"They'll wait for me." Erma shifted her gaze to the back of the audience and her dark eyes went round. "Don't tell me. Is *that* your date?"

Logan was approaching them, and he only had eyes for Bliss. Heat spread from her neck to her cheeks even as another odd noise made the skin on her spine crawl.

"Forget it," Erma whispered. "You don't have to say a thing."

The next screech was earsplitting.

Logan's gaze jerked to the ceiling. "Bliss, get—"

The sound of collapsing metal cut off his words. Horrified, Bliss looked up to see an entire section of the steel lighting grid swinging down at them as if in slow motion. An adrenaline rush made her move faster than she ever had in her life. She grabbed Erma and pushed with all her might. They both went sprawling onto the studio floor as the steel bars crashed mere inches away. Metal parts and splintered glass from the lights pelted them both.

"Bliss, Erma—are you all right?" Logan shouted as he ran onto the stage and hopped over the fallen grid. "My God, you both could have been killed."

"I heard someone back there," Bliss gasped, rising to lean on one hand and pointing to the stained-glass window with the other. When she realized he was bending over to help her up, she yelled, "I'm fine. Don't let him get away!"

Hesitating only a second, Logan flew toward the backstage area.

"You think someone did this on purpose? Someone wanted to kill us? Or you?" Erma said, partly dazed.

Before Bliss could decide how to respond, pandemonium broke loose. People were descending on them from every direction and shouting questions.

"Erma, let me do the talking, *please*," Bliss whispered as she got to her feet. Though the other woman nodded, she didn't look too happy. "I promise I'll explain later. You are all right, aren't you?"

"Just bruised." She took Bliss's hand and rose shakily. "Everything's in working order."

The next few minutes went by in a blur. Crew members helped them pick splinters of broken glass from their clothing while others started to clean up the mess on the stage. Someone suggested calling a doctor, but neither Bliss nor Erma felt that was necessary. And while Bliss fielded questions as best she could, Dean and Joelle appeared, seemingly out of nowhere.

"Bliss, darlin', what happened here?"

"You aren't hurt, are you?" Dean asked, his tone sounding worried.

She told Dean and his mother nothing different than she had the others. She had no idea what happened. Somehow the grid just gave. And they were very lucky to have escaped injury. She kept her expression and voice natural, even while wondering why Dean hadn't met her after rehearsal as he'd said he would.

Had he been the one she'd heard behind the scenery? Could he somehow have staged this "accident"?

Aghast at the thought, she was glad when Logan showed up and took the situation in hand. "I'll take these ladies someplace quiet where they can calm down. All of you pitch in and get this mess cleaned up."

Several members of the crew were already removing lights from the grid while others had fetched brooms and dustpans for the shattered glass.

The cameraman named Jim asked, "Are we still going to do the broadcast?"

"No," Logan said as Dean contradicted him with a vehement, "Yes."

The two men glared at each other. Bliss could feel the tension emanating from Logan though he wasn't quite touching her. She wondered if he, too, suspected his cousin.

But Dean's was the voice of reason. "We have several hundred people waiting out in the lobby and parking lot. There are hundreds of thousands more at home expecting a live broadcast. I'm not going to disappoint any of them. We'll have to hurry because we don't have much time to clean up and reset lights."

"Dean, what's wrong with you? Are you allowing your ambitions to override common decency? These two women could have been killed. We can transmit a re-run."

"You're just like your interfering mother. Stay out of this, Logan!"

Joelle swayed toward her nephew as she spoke. Alcohol fumes reached Bliss before Dean put a restraining hand on his mother's arm.

"Please, Mother, I can handle this." To Logan he said, "I plan to dedicate this program to the Lord in thanks that no one was seriously injured."

With a sound of disgust, Logan whipped away from him and led Bliss and Erma into the empty control room.

"Did you see anyone?" Bliss asked anxiously as soon as they were alone.

"No one, but that grid couldn't have fallen by itself. Someone must have loosened the hangers ahead of time and then set that one end free when you heard the first noise. The weight of the equipment itself did the rest of the damage," he said with certainty. "I found one of the loading-dock doors open a crack. He or she must have gotten out that way."

"If the guilty party isn't still in the studio."

"All right. Time out. What's going on?" Erma demanded to know. "Bliss, you promised...."

Even sensing she could trust Erma, Bliss didn't want to tell her everything, which would put her in more danger. "After the first rehearsal, some goon attacked me outside."

"Did you call the police?"

"No. And I don't want to now, either. Please. If someone has something against me personally, I don't want to involve the ministry. This wouldn't make good press. You understand, don't you?''

"Not really, but I won't say anything for the moment if that's what you really want," Erma promised. "Who do you think is doing this to you?"

"I don't know."

"If you feel up to leaving, I can have someone drive you home," Logan offered.

"No way. I'm joining my friends at the ice-cream parlor and eating twice as much as I'd intended to. A person never knows when she might be ordering her last banana split.''

Though Erma had obviously meant it as a joke, no one was laughing.

"The least I can do is see that you get to your car safely," Logan insisted. He turned to Bliss. "You'll be all right if I leave you for a few minutes?"

"I'm fine. Really." Just shaken up and frightened, she added silently. And nothing was going to change that. She waved them on. "Go ahead." Then, when they got to the control-room door, Bliss said, "Erma, I'm really sorry. I didn't mean to involve you."

"Hey, we're friends. I think you should let the police handle this, but I don't think you're going to do that, so you be careful...and if there's anything I can do to help, you ask."

"This is my problem."

"Well, somebody just made it mine, too."

With that, Erma and Logan left studio control. Bliss took a deep breath, sat in a chair at the lit camera-switching console and let herself sag. Listening to the hypnotic electronic hum of equipment she knew nothing about, she stared out the tinted windows to the studio.

The stage floor had already been cleared of debris. Dean was standing in the middle with Osmond, undoubtedly explaining what had happened, while technicians on platform ladders were adding and resetting lights. Off to one side, Lurlene and Joelle seemed to be having an intense argument.

Bliss closed her eyes, but as if her brain were a video screen, it replayed the grid falling...in slow motion. Shaking her head as if she could dislodge the memory, she opened her eyes. Maybe she wasn't so all right and shock was setting in.

The blank screens of the monitors in front of her suddenly burst alive with light as technicians on the floor uncapped their cameras. All six of them moved in for close-ups of Dean or Osmond, who turned this way and that as the lighting people made final adjustments.

She wondered if Dean's was the face of a criminal—and a potential murderer.

Studying the two men on the black-and-white monitors, Bliss once more speculated if they might be more alike than Osmond knew. In the studio, Dean's natural shyness and insecurity were as well hidden as they had been the day before when he'd made his proposal to her in his uncle's study.

The younger man had the right look—Osmond's—as she'd noted then. And something else she couldn't quite pin down nagged her.

Before she could contemplate further, the control-room door burst open with a bang. She rose and turned from the monitors, expecting to see Logan.

"I just heard what happened," Hope said, her expression anxious as she approached the console. "They said you were okay, but I wanted to make sure for myself."

Feeling awkward because of what she'd surmised about Hope or Dean having an affair, Bliss held on to the back of the chair for support. "My knees are a little shaky and I expect I'll have a few bruises, but other than that..."

"Well, I just wanted to see for myself," Hope said, giving Bliss a quick hug. "I can't tell you how sorry I am this happened."

She seemed about to say something more but changed her mind when the door opened again, this time to let in Logan.

"Listen, I have to go," Hope said. "Dean always needs me to be with him in his dressing room while he's preparing for a broadcast."

"Don't worry about me. I'll be fine."

But watching the other woman rush across the room and give Logan a stricken look before exiting, Bliss wondered if *she* was all right.

"What was that all about?" Logan asked.

"She wanted to make sure I wasn't hurt."

"Hmm."

"She did!" Bliss was too deeply exhausted, too newly traumatized to argue. "Logan, about tonight—"

"You're coming to my place. We can leave right now. Vern will take over for me."

"I'm not hungry."

"Then you don't have to eat, but you're not staying in that apartment alone."

The meaning of his words sank in immediately. "Well, I'm not staying at your place."

"And I'm not going to argue. Either you agree to spend the night with me, or I call the police right now and tell them this wasn't a freak accident as everyone thinks." As if he were ready to carry out his threat, Logan lifted the receiver of the wall phone. "I should call the police anyway."

More deeply frightened than she cared to admit, not wanting to be alone anyway, Bliss put a staying hand on his. "Which of us gets the floor?"

Logan gave her a disgusted look as he replaced the receiver on its hook. Is that what she was worried about?

"We'll toss a coin."

"All right. As long as we have that straight."

"You never give over, do you? You've got to be the tough woman if it kills you. Well, if you're not more careful, that attitude just might be enough to do the trick."

LOGAN LEANED BACK from the white pine table and stared at his reluctant dinner companion. "Sure you don't want another pork chop?" He speared one with his fork and waved it under Bliss's nose.

"I told you I wasn't hungry."

"For an unhungry person, you did yourself proud." He replaced the chop on the platter, which he placed in the refrigerator. "How about dessert or a glass of wine?"

Her brows shot up. "You drink?"

"Occasionally. You don't approve. Because of my father?"

"Because of mine. Dad drank too much."

"Well, I don't, so don't compare us." Amused by her mutinous expression, which Bliss had been wearing since they'd left the studio, Logan took a bottle of wine from the refrigerator, then found the corkscrew in one of the counter drawers. "There must be some reason you keep trying to deny what you feel for me."

"For starters, there's my sister."

"I explained how it was with us." He sensed she believed him, though she might not want to. He opened the wine and backtracked to a cabinet where he kept a couple of stemmed glasses. "I think you're afraid to give a man your love or believe he could love you as you deserve."

"When did you become a psychoanalyst?" Bliss asked, her tone caustic.

"You're the one who told me your father shut you and your sister out emotionally after your mother died."

"I didn't say that exactly."

"You didn't have to."

Logan could tell he'd hit a nerve—not that he had intended to this time.

What he wanted was to spend a nice, relaxed evening with the women he loved, but she was strung so tight she might snap if he touched her. He wanted her to melt in his arms, to make love with him in front of the roaring fire. Even though they'd met such a short while ago, Logan felt as if he'd known Bliss for a lifetime. In his heart, he knew she was the right woman for him, and he was ready to show her how he felt.

He filled two glasses and set one in front of her. "Have some wine. A couple of sips will make you feel better."

"Finding Melody alive and well and getting back to Indianapolis with her is the only thing that'll make me feel better."

Logan raised his own drink. "Thanks a lot. Makes me feel real good."

He took a sip and moved over to the couch where he made himself comfortable and put his stockinged feet up on the rough-hewn coffee table facing the fire. The dishes could wait until morning, as far as he was concerned. He didn't know how long he'd been staring into the fire when he realized Bliss was standing over him, her glass clutched between both hands.

"You haven't been doing this for me," she said. "You're protecting your own interests."

"I might have started out doing that. But that was a long time ago."

"Less than a week."

"A week can seem like forever."

She dropped to the thick area rug in front of the fire. He watched her profile as she took a sip of the wine. Dressed in a flowing pale gold dress almost the same shade as the hair spilling around her shoulders, she looked like an angel.

"I feel as if my whole world has changed," she murmured.

A ray of hope teased him. "What are we talking about? Are you admitting there is an us? Give me one reason why there can't be."

"I have too many doubts about the ministry, and the life here holds no appeal for me. I'm not your mother or Hope. I'm simply not the right woman . . ."

As her words trailed off, Logan placed his glass on the table and slipped to the floor next to her. "I'm not a minister and I don't have to live here."

"But you're considering taking over for your father. What if Dean is the person who's responsible for everything? Then Osmond would have no one to turn to but you."

Logan finally admitted to himself something he'd known all along. "I would still have to say no to Father. I'm not the stuff of which ministers are made."

"Why not? Because you like fast cars and good wine . . . and women? Those things don't make you unworthy."

"But my heart does. I'm not a self-sacrificing person."

Setting her glass down on the floor, Bliss turned her head toward the fire and stared into the flames as if in them she could see the future. If only she could believe him. He didn't have to clean up his act as much as he pretended. He was a good man, in some ways a better man than his father. As for self-sacrificing, he'd almost sacrificed his life to protect his family. How much more proof of commitment could anyone make?

"Bliss, I wish I could calm all your fears about who and what I am or may become, but only you can do that by having faith in your own judgment. You always have such trust in yourself, in your own abilities. I love you. I think you could feel the same way about me if you let yourself."

"I already do." The words were out of her mouth before she had time to consider them. She'd been afraid to name the emotion before; now she was afraid not to. What if something happened to one of them and this was the only chance she ever had to tell him? "I love you, too, Logan."

His touch made her turn away from the fire and into his arms. Their kiss was bittersweet because of the emotions it aroused. He'd been accurate when he's said she had always trusted herself in everything but love. She didn't want one night with him; only a lifetime would satisfy her.

Logan ended the kiss, pulled her tightly against him, murmured her name, his lips against her hair. He pressed her back into the carpet and settled himself next to her, then began a slow, exquisite exploration of her body. He watched her face intently as he slid his hand down her belly and lower to pull up her skirt and rub the polished cotton against her thighs.

"Shall I find that coin now?" Logan asked softly as he made her legs part with a more intimate touch. When Bliss looked at him in dazed puzzlement, he added, "The one that decides which of us sleeps on the floor."

His invitation was clear even as he gave her an out. She could run scared or she could have faith . . . in him.

"We could both sleep on the floor together."

Logan's slow smile made her melt inside. She watched his face as he began undoing the tiny buttons holding the front of her dress together. His expression was the most erotic thing she'd ever seen.

He undressed her and she in turn helped him shed his trousers and long-sleeved cotton sweater. She tried to put everything but him out of her mind as he slipped over her. Tangling her fingers in his curly hair, she brought his face closer, studying it. She closed her eyes when they kissed, and he explored her mouth and her body more fully.

Bliss let herself go completely and welcomed the man she loved in the most intimate of ways. Then, fused with him, she forgot everything but the physical passion that made her moan and shudder and feel more complete than she ever had in her life. Logan was an exquisite and demanding lover, one who expected only as much as he gave. But when the moment of truth had passed, and they lay in each other's arms, chests heaving, bodies sated and damp, the uncertainty of their love was still there to haunt her.

As if sensing her discomfort, he drew her closer and wrapped his warm body around hers protectively. She smiled up at him, kissed him passionately, but inside she was more afraid than she'd ever been.

Could their feelings for each other last a lifetime, or would the truth, when finally revealed, have the power to destroy what they'd just found?

UNABLE TO CHOOSE a single chapter and verse of the Bible that would say it all, the author of the threats began typing the final note.

To Osmond Wright—
  Matthew 5.6. *Blessed are they who hunger and thirst after righteousness: for they shall be filled.*
  Judgment day has arrived, Osmond, and you have been found guilty. Beg the Lord for forgiveness.
  Luke 6.30. *Give to every man that asketh of thee; and of him that taketh away thy goods ask not for their return.*
  To me, you'll pay for your transgressions here on earth—one millions dollars in cash.

Pausing for a moment, the blackmailer thought about the most appropriate time and place for the exchange and added that to the missive. It was really too bad the pleasure couldn't be drawn out longer so that the televangelist would know exactly how it felt to be manipulated for what seemed like a lifetime.

Still, the author couldn't help but be well satisfied: in less than twenty-four hours, Osmond Wright's world would collapse around him.

## Chapter Twelve

The following evening, after checking in at the dressing room and enlisting Erma's aid in private, Bliss cornered Logan in his office. "I have to get into the parsonage while your family is here at the broadcast."

His brow furrowed. "What are you talking about?"

"I want to search your father's study."

"Are you crazy? You can't do that."

"Don't tell me what I can or cannot do!"

Odd how she could glare at him straight in the eye when she had a cause to defend. That morning, she'd hardly been able to look at Logan, not because they'd made love, but because she was afraid that her heart would break when they found the truth. If he had sensed her discomfort that morning, he hadn't let on. At her request, he'd taken her back to her apartment without suggesting they investigate further.

Had he thought she would give up just because she'd admitted her love for him?

"You're supposed to be here in the studio—" Logan was saying "—as one of the Singing Angels."

"And I will be. After our opening numbers, the choir will leave the stage while your father gives his sermon and interviews his guest, and Dean promotes *The Osmond*

*Wright Workaday Bible*. That's when I'll slip out the back. I'll have plenty of time."

"Forty minutes."

"That's enough."

"And what if Nardini or someone wonders about your absence?"

"Erma will cover for me. She'll say that I'm in the ladies' room with a nervous stomach. I may have one at that."

"Let's be sensible here," Logan pleaded. He rose and circled his desk toward her. "What do you think you're going to accomplish by searching my father's study?"

"Maybe I'll find another threat," she said, trying not to let his nearness affect her.

Actually she wasn't even sure what to look for. She just knew that somehow, the threat to his father and her sister's disappearance were linked.

"When are you going to give up?" Logan asked.

"You mean quit?"

"I mean leave the investigation in the hands of the police."

Bliss told herself not to panic. He kept talking about the police, but so far he hadn't called them. She needed to buy herself some more time.

"Monday," she said. "Give me until noon on Monday, please. I have this feeling that we're so close—"

"That's not surprising since between us we've experienced three murder attempts in one week." Logan moved toward her and slipped a hand around her neck. "What if the killer is watching you, planning to go after you again, no mistakes this time?"

Bliss felt the blood rush from her face but she would not show her fear to him. She stood fast. "I'm going to do this. With or without your help, I'm going to search your father's office.''

"My help." He dropped the hand and backed off. "What am I supposed to do from here? I can't come with you. Yesterday was an exception, but I can't make another excuse to be gone during the broadcast."

"Keep an eye on your family and make sure no one comes back to the parsonage unexpectedly."

Logan sighed. "All right. I'll do that. But if you don't find anything, you and I will go to the police first thing in the morning and tell them everything we've found, or even suspected."

Bliss knew better than to argue. She'd gotten her time. "Agreed. I'd better get back to the dressing room."

When she was halfway to the door, Logan said, "Go in through the living-room window on the east side. There's a rose trellis. You don't weigh much, so you can use it as a ladder."

"Thanks," she said, smiling at him for the first time since she'd forced the confrontation.

"And check your watch. You'd better be back in the waiting area in your robes in forty minutes."

"I will."

"One more thing."

"What?"

Logan trapped her against the door. "Be careful." He covered her mouth and kissed her deeply so that she was breathless by the time he raised his head. "And remember that I love you."

"I love you, too," she whispered, giving him another quick kiss before slipping out the door into master control.

Happy that he was sticking by her despite his own loyalties, Bliss rushed through the equipment area into the hallway that led to the dressing rooms. Erma was waiting for her with the shoulder bag Bliss had left for safe-keeping. It contained clothes from her sister's closet.

"Everything all right?" Bliss asked softly.

"Everyone's been too busy to notice you've been gone."

"Good."

Taking the bag from Erma, she slipped her gold robe from its hanger. Once in the ladies' room, she changed into a pair of Melody's jeans and a short-sleeved golden-brown shirt. She pulled the belt tight and rolled up the ends of the pants to her calves. Though a bit large, the outfit would allow her to sneak through the night with ease and agility more than any of her pastel dresses. Nothing she could do about the shoes, however. Melody's feet were far larger than her own. She would have to make do wearing heels.

The door creaked open. "Bliss, you'd better hurry," Erma called. "They want us lined up backstage in two minutes."

"I'll be right there."

Folding her dress and stuffing it into the shoulder bag, she slipped into the choir gown and ran a comb through her loose hair. She rushed through the empty dressing room, pausing only to set the bag under a makeup counter.

Then she entered the hallway, quickly caught up to the other women and took her place in line. She could hear the noisy audience even from backstage. Erma winked as Bliss glanced back at her. She felt as if her stomach were clutching, but she didn't know which made her more nervous: the thought of searching the parsonage or singing on live television.

Paul Nardini didn't give her long to think about it, however, for he began ushering his choir members on stage. Being the shortest meant Bliss stood in the first row. The audience hushed with their entrance. She stared down at her sheet music.

"Quiet on the set!" the floor manager shouted a moment later. "One minute until airtime."

Her nerves on edge, she silently counted down with him.

"Thirty seconds," the man warned as Osmond slipped behind his darkened stage pulpit.

The spotlights slowly came up with the rising voices of the Singing Angels. Bliss felt sweat gathering under her clothes while her throat went dry. She only hoped she could make it through these first two numbers. The lights blinded her so she couldn't see the audience and the red tally light on top of the camera reminded her she was on national television. Looking down, she was hardly able to concentrate on her sheet music. Somehow she made it through the first number anyway.

Then Osmond was introduced. He greeted his audience, made his opening statements and turned the show back over to the choir. Bliss made it through the second hymn, as well. And then the focus shifted back to the televangelist who was about to begin his sermon.

The choir slipped backstage at exactly seven minutes after eight. Giving herself a few minutes leeway, she should be back in the studio and in her robes by eight-forty-two.

Bliss lagged behind as some members of the choir positioned themselves where they could see the stage, while others headed for the dressing room. Erma caught up to her and together they ducked into the inner loading-dock area. She slipped off the robe and handed it to the other woman who folded it neatly and slid it into a dark plastic bag.

"I'll leave the bag behind this garbage can," Erma whispered as Bliss clipped her hair out of the way. "How soon will you be back?"

"I'll try for eight-forty-two."

"That's cutting it close."

The two women hugged and Bliss shot out the door, knowing that Erma would leave it unlatched for her. She scooted down the steps and headed for the hillside, pausing only to take off her heels once she hit the grass. Then, using the shelter of the trees as cover, she ran across the grounds toward the mansion that glowed dimly in the distance.

She didn't allow herself to think about the area she was entering . . . about what had almost happened there.

By the time she reached the east window of the parsonage, she was out of breath and a stitch made her side ache. Ignoring the discomfort, she dropped her shoes at the bottom of the trellis and, heedful of the thorny shoots of the blooming roses, climbed up the few feet to the sill. The window was barely open. Carefully she edged it higher, hooked a leg over the ledge and slipped inside the darkened room.

Bliss paused a moment to catch her breath and allow her heartbeat to slow. A dim light beckoned from the hallway, and she was relieved when her eyes adjusted to her surroundings. She listened for any untoward sounds in the house, then checked her watch. Eight-fourteen. Twenty-one minutes to search the study, and she could make it back to the studio at an easy lope in the remaining seven minutes. She would hardly be out of breath.

If only her nerves would calm down.

Quietly, just in case anyone was around to hear, she tiptoed to the study where she pulled the shade and closed the door before turning on a light. Her pulse threaded unevenly, then settled down. Where to start? The desk drawers. Mindful of each second that ticked away, she pulled out the first one and began her search.

PRAYING THAT BLISS wouldn't find anything to incriminate his father or anyone else in the family, Logan kept a close eye on the monitors in master control. His father and Dean were in place on stage, his mother sat with Hope and Gregory in the audience, and Joelle was watching Osmond from the wings. All were within a camera's view.

"This evening I will read the words of Jesus Christ, Our Lord, taken from the Gospel of St. Luke," his father was saying. He paused, head bowed, and gathered his forces before looking straight into the close-up camera. "'Judge not, and ye shall not be judged: condemn not, and ye shall not be condemned: forgive, and ye shall be forgiven.'"

A chill shot through Logan.

*Do unto others . . . look to your own sins.*

He hadn't forgotten the missive, and neither had his father. Osmond was addressing the threat directly. His father didn't know he was dealing with some desperate soul who was willing to kill to achieve his or her ends.

He never should have allowed Bliss to carry through with her foolish plan. What if . . .

A furtive movement on one of the monitors caught his eye. Joelle, backing out of the stage wings as if she were leaving, no doubt to return to the parsonage. He didn't have to check his watch to know that Bliss hadn't completed her search. She'd barely had enough time to get across the grounds.

"Vern, can you take over for a few minutes?" he asked his assistant engineer.

"Sure, boss, what's up?"

Logan was already racing across master control toward the hallway. "Nothing I can't handle."

He caught up to his aunt in the dimly lit loading dock as she approached the door. She jerked around, then sighed in relief. "Logan, you startled me."

Did she have some reason to be so jumpy? "Sorry."

She turned back to the door and pushed. "Someone left this door open. You'd better talk to your people about being more careful."

"Thanks for telling me." He followed her outside, hoping to stall her with conversation. "I have a headache. I thought some fresh air would help."

Joelle was already lighting a cigarette with a shaky hand. "I need a drink. Want to join me?"

"No, thanks. I have to stick around until we're off the air." Sensing she was about to leave, he brought up her favorite topic. "Dean is turning into quite a televangelist. He's come a long way from the shy kid I used to know."

"He's brilliant, really," Joelle said with motherly pride. And then, bitterly, she added, "Not that Ossie will ever give him credit for any of his ideas."

"Father will come around."

"I wonder. He's had years." She took a nervous drag on the cigarette and blew the smoke away from Logan. "Ossie treats him no better than he would a stranger sometimes."

"Father can be too stubborn. That's why I was thinking about leaving." A picture of Bliss came to him. "One of the reasons. I guess the only way to prove that I don't want to be his successor is to leave the ministry, for good, this time.''

Joelle gave him a searching look. ''You would do that for Dean?''

''For all of us, including you. You know I love both of you.''

The garish blue light from the building made her look slightly haggard, older than her years. Her expression stricken, eyes glassy with unshed tears, Joelle turned away from him and grasped the steel railing.

Logan sensed the upheaval his words had caused in her and realized he had never before told her how much he cared. He remembered his aunt, not as a pushy woman who smoked and drank too much, but as she had been decades before, when he and Dean were kids. She'd been so beautiful, so vibrant, so filled with good humor that he'd been enchanted by her. What had happened to change her? She was now filled with such bitterness and loneliness.

He touched her shoulder. ''Are you all right?''

''Joelle is always all right. Tough. It's Lurlene who needs to be taken care of, to be treated with delicacy, to be worshiped....'' She threw the cigarette onto the pavement and ground it under her toe. ''I'm sorry, Logan, that was not fair of me. I know you love your mother. Funny, in spite of everything, *I* still love her.''

With that enigmatic statement, she started down the stairs.

''Aunt Joelle, where are you going?''

''To have that drink.'' She glanced back at him and a bitter smile played across her lips. ''While I'm at it, I'll have a drink for you, too.''

Watching her become one with the night, Logan uneasily wondered what all that had been about. He checked his watch and swore softly. His aunt was heading for the parsonage. No doubt she would arrive before Bliss could make her escape.

No LUCK. She had searched every nook and cranny of Osmond's study. If there was a clue to be found, it had surely escaped her.

She opened the middle desk drawer and sorted through the papers. An ancient picture stared up at her. She lifted the black-and-white photograph. A much younger Osmond had his arms around the shoulders of two boys—Logan and Dean. Something about the picture bothered her, but Bliss couldn't quite put her finger on what. She returned it to the desk, and in doing so, knocked the blotter out of position.

A sliver of gray caught her eye.

Lifting the blotter, she found an envelope of gray bond stationery, exactly like the paper on which the "do unto others" warning had been typed. Another threat? Heart pounding with excitement, she removed the envelope from its hiding place and pulled out the contents. Unfolding the paper, she glanced at the few lines scrawled in a familiar handwriting—that of a left-handed person.

Melody!

Her breath caught as she read the message, which began with the day's date.

Dear Osmond,
   I need your help desperately. Please come to me at The Lord is My Shepherd Motel right after tonight's broadcast. I'll be waiting for you. I pray you will not fail me in this, my time of need.

Melody

With nerveless fingers, Bliss managed to refold the message and put the note in her back jeans' pocket. Joy at knowing her sister was alive was tempered by fear and suspicion. What kind of trouble was she in? And why was she turning to Osmond for help?

It was eight-thirty-three, time to head back. She could think while she ran. Returning the room to its original darkened state, Bliss cracked open the door and listened to make sure the coast was clear before venturing forth. She'd barely gotten into the living room, when she heard the outer door open and close. Staccato clicks made by a woman's heels as she walked across the marble entrance made Bliss find a hiding place behind a chair near the open window.

The woman advanced down the hall, coming even closer. When a soft light at the other end of the room went on, Bliss was sure the game was up. Then a cabinet hinge groaned and the familiar sound of crystal revealed the woman's identity. Joelle had come back to the house for a drink. Perhaps Dean's mother would take the alcohol to her room. Footsteps again. She risked peeking around the chair just as Joelle set down her glass on an end table, picked up the telephone and dialed a number.

Eight-thirty-six—one minute past her deadline to be heading back for the studio. Bliss began to feel clammy. She had to get out of there and fast.

"Hello, Walders? You were supposed to call me this morning with your report." Joelle paused, then said, "I'm not paying you to make excuses."

Bliss sneaked another look as the other woman turned her back to the windows. Seconds—no, minutes—were flying by. Her stomach churned with nervous tension, but she had to take a chance on escape. Edging away from the chair in a crouch, she silently made her way to the window and over the ledge, all the while keeping an eye on Logan's aunt.

"What?" Joelle cried as Bliss blindly felt for a footing on the trellis. "The Griffith woman is Melody Sawyer's sister?"

Startled by her words, Bliss missed the trellis completely and would have fallen to the ground if a strong arm hadn't wrapped around her waist while a firm hand clamped over her mouth. She stiffened only a second before thrashing her arms and legs as she tried to fight her captor.

"Bliss! Shh," Logan hissed. "We've got to get you back to the studio."

Filled with relief, she went limp. He set her down, took her by the hand and began pulling her across the lawn.

"Wait!" she whispered, dragging her heels in the grass. "My shoes."

"Where?"

She freed herself and found them where she'd discarded them under the trellis. Then, hand in hand, she and Logan made a mad dash across the lawn and into the shadow of the trees. Though she had a lot to tell him, explanations would have to wait. She was already almost out of breath. He was forcing her to run faster than she had before. She fairly flew over the grounds and toward the studio building.

A few minutes later, they entered through the loading-dock door. Waiting anxiously with the gown, Erma helped her slip into the garment, then buttoned it up while Bliss freed her hair.

"I have to get back to master control," Logan said softly. "Are you going to make it?"

Not sparing her breath on an answer, she nodded and he took off.

"Where's that comb?" Erma asked.

Bliss drew it out of her back pocket and smoothed her hair as best she could. "Do I look all right?" she asked with a wheeze.

"You'll do. Come on."

By the time they entered the hallway, Paul Nardini was already looking for them. "Where have you two been? Everyone's in place on stage."

"She's been sick," Erma told him. "Stage fright. But she'll be all right now."

"Oh, Lord, that's all we need. A Singing Angel getting sick in front of a live audience."

"I'll be fine," Bliss assured him as Erma dragged her to the opening in the flats.

Quietly they slipped into place as the choir received its cue for the next number. This time, she had to fake singing. She was short of breath and her mind was spinning with unanswered questions.

Why was Melody in trouble? Was her sister really Osmond's lover? Why had Joelle been checking on *her*? And how did Dean fit into the picture?

Her time for speculation was running out.

AFTER THE BROADCAST, Bliss quickly changed back into her dress, thanked an inquisitive Erma for her help and promised to keep her posted, then went on to master control in search of Logan. Her pulse skittered. She had so much to tell him and didn't know where to begin.

When she found him, she said, "Can we talk?"

"Vern just went outside to have a smoke and a cup of coffee." He moved closer as if to take her in his arms. "He'll be back in a few minutes."

Bliss put a hand on his chest. "We can't wait. Melody is in danger."

"What are you talking about?"

"I found this in your father's study, under the desk blotter," she said, handing him the note.

"Why didn't you tell me you'd found something?" he asked, frowning at her.

"You didn't give me a chance. I was lucky I could breathe by the time we got back here."

"At least we know Melody is alive." His frown deepened as he read. "What kind of trouble could she be in?"

"I have no idea, but we have to get to that motel as soon as possible."

"This paper. . ." Logan refolded the note and handed it back to her. "Isn't this written on the same stationery you found in your sister's Bible?"

Bliss didn't like the tone of his voice or the intent way he was looking at her. That she, herself, had wondered about the stationery didn't soothe her irritation with him.

"Yes, it's the same," she said stiffly. "What's your point?"

"Maybe Melody sent the threat to my father."

"Talk about grasping at straws!" She held on to her temper with difficulty. "Melody is the one in trouble."

"So she says."

"Are you saying you don't believe her?"

"Let's say I don't know what to believe anymore. So maybe it's time to call in the police."

"How could you even suggest such a thing before we find out what's going on?"

"By the time we find out, it may be too late."

"It'll be too late if we don't hurry." Bliss shoved the note into a side pocket of her bag, then fought with the zipper. "You said that if I didn't find anything we'd go to the police on Monday at noon. Well, it's not that time, and I did find something." She jerked the zipper closed and gave him a triumphant look. "Are you coming with me?"

"I can't leave until Vern gets back."

"Your precious equipment is more important than a woman's life?"

"We don't know that Melody's life is being threatened."

She glared at him. "Why are you being so unreasonable?"

"I'm not. Everyone has gone except Vern who'll be here all night. He'll be back in a moment."

"Maybe you're afraid that you might learn the truth about what you've been dreading most—that your father isn't some saint, but a human with faults like the rest of us."

Now Logan was getting angry. His posture was stiff and he practically glowered at her.

"My father is the best man—"

"My sister is in trouble! I'm going to her. *Now.* I'll ask one last time. Are you coming with me?"

"Be reasonable."

"I don't feel like being reasonable." She stalked past him toward studio control.

"Bliss! Don't do this. You might get hurt."

"I am already hurt. And disappointed."

Why couldn't he see that his father wasn't perfect? He would have to open his eyes eventually, she thought, entering the studio control room. Let him live under a cloud of delusion. She didn't care what her sister might have gotten herself into this time. She loved Melody and always would.

Three quarters of the way through the control room, a furtive movement from the studio caught her eye. Stopping, she stared out the tinted windows to the studio floor only to see Osmond Wright clandestinely glancing over his shoulder as he moved through the empty, dimly lit room.

What was he doing there at ten o'clock when the facility was deserted except for the night engineer? He should be on his way to Melody. And the leather satchel he was carrying—blackmail money? The thought came out of nowhere, yet Bliss knew she'd hit on the answer.

The threat had been a lead-in to blackmail!

Osmond slipped backstage behind the pulpit area. She began to get uneasy but waited and watched. A moment later, he came back out—empty-handed. He glanced around once more, then rushed across the floor toward the main doors.

Torn between going after him and wanting to find out for certain what was in the case, Bliss hesitated. Instinct told her the satchel was filled with money, but she wanted to see for herself. She set down her shoulder bag and entered the studio, then stood still in the shadows when she noticed another movement, this time from the audience.

A dark-clothed figure glided from the seating area to the studio floor.

Bliss knew she was looking at the blackmailer.

Without hesitating, she slipped out of her heels as the mysterious person disappeared backstage exactly as Osmond had. She hurried across the poorly lit studio and into the silent, pitch-black prop area where she played a lone game of hide-and-seek with her quarry. The blackmailer had no reason to suspect she was there.

A soft scuffling noise gave her direction. Pulse racing with anticipation, Bliss moved by instinct, slowly and silently. She felt her way through the maze of stage pieces. Another noise indicated she was even closer. A sense of triumph warred with caution. Her eagerness to reveal the blackmailer's identity won.

Lunging forward, she grew careless and her bare foot collided with the sharp edge of a platform. A pained gasp escaped her. With a low curse, her quarry scrambled through the area away from her sight. The loading-dock door! Bliss was closer. She retraced her steps to cut off escape.

In the hallway, the dark-garbed person who was carrying the satchel came from the other direction.

"Why don't you just give up?" Bliss yelled as the other person ducked away from her. "You're not going to get away with this."

The blackmailer switched back and Bliss guessed the person would try to escape through the studio.

Who was it? There hadn't been enough light to tell. She followed and played a short game of tag in the dark around the set pieces. The game came to an abrupt halt when her quarry shoved a fake wall, which came flying down on top of Bliss, stopping her temporarily. Luckily this flat was light, made of painted canvas stretched around a wooden frame.

As she freed herself, Bliss smelled the faint scent of roses.

A woman.

She'd been correct then. There were two of them. A man and a woman. Was it Joelle? Bliss remembered the bottle of Laviana Rose Water. Then again, Logan's aunt made purchases for other members of the household. Had she bought the scent for someone else...?

Speculation was getting her nowhere; confrontation would reveal the woman's identity.

She scrambled to her feet and caught up with the blackmailer before the other woman got to the stairs. Bliss grabbed the satchel with both hands, tugged hard and flew backward. She landed on her rear and the satchel sailed out of her grasp. Keeping her face averted, the other woman lunged after it.

"Oh, no you don't!" Bliss yelled.

Rather than trying to keep the loot away from the blackmailer, Bliss went for the knit cap. It came off easily in her hand, and the woman's hair spilled around the dark-clad shoulders.

Bliss caught her breath as, at last, the blackmailer faced her.

## Chapter Thirteen

Sorry that he'd let Bliss go as he had, Logan left master control as soon as Vern returned from his break. He intended to get to that motel as quickly as his car would take him. He was halfway through the smaller control room before he became aware of the struggle in the studio.

On the floor, while someone in black went after a leather case, Bliss reached out and snatched away the person's knit cap. The attacker didn't have to turn around for him to identify her. The hair was a giveaway. What the hell was going on?

And why was Hope pulling a gun on Bliss?

As he was about to find out for himself, Logan froze. Rushing into the studio might make her pull the trigger. He spotted a microphone boom nearby. With his heart in his throat, he flicked on the board switch and raised the volume so he could hear what they were saying. He had to do something, but what?

" . . . knew you were unhappy, but—"

"You should have let well enough alone, Bliss."

"I never figured you would resort to blackmail . . . or worse."

The word "blackmail" triggered Logan to action. At the camera-control unit, he brought up the iris on Jim's camera. Bless the forgetful man—he hadn't capped the lens. There was a wide shot of the two women.

"I didn't mean for there to be any violence," Hope said, her tone almost convincing Logan she was sincere. "I like you and I'm fond of Logan."

Realizing Hope didn't seem anxious to shoot Bliss and run off, Logan picked up the phone and dialed master control, at the same time punching up the camera as the outgoing feed from the switching console.

"But Osmond deserves to pay," Hope was saying. "He ruined my life."

"He couldn't have done that alone. Why didn't you stand up to him?"

When Vern picked up the phone at the other end, Logan told him, "Kill the prerecorded videotape *now* and route the studio feed live over CLN."

"Got it, boss," Vern said.

Logan hung up and checked the CLN monitor as the video went wild, then settled in to the shot of the studio. The picture wasn't great, but the players were recognizable even in the low light. About to enter the studio himself, he hesitated when he heard what Hope was saying.

"You don't know the great Osmond Wright very well, do you? He puts on this holier-than-thou front and manipulates you into thinking his way. It took me a while to realize what he was doing to my husband, what Osmond had been doing to him even before Dean was born."

What was that supposed to mean? Logan wondered.

Getting to her feet Bliss distracted him from pursuing that line of thought. Hope backed off, out of her reach. Logan prayed Bliss wouldn't do anything foolish. That gun in Hope's hand looked deadly enough. For a moment, Bliss stared straight at the camera. Then she shot a quick glance at the control-room window before turning back to Hope.

"Why didn't you fight for what you wanted?" Bliss asked.

Logan was sure she'd seen the glowing red tally light on top of the camera; she knew a signal was being transmitted.

"The more I tried to get Dean to stand on his own, away from Osmond, the more determined he was to please the old hypocrite. The situation got even worse when Logan came home. Finally I just gave up. I decided to find happiness where I could."

"By taking the ministry's money, or by having an affair?"

Hope started. "Both. Dean loved me once, enough to fight for me. According to Osmond, I was Louisville trash. My family was just plain poor, like he was once. Dean defied him and married me. He was my knight in shining armor until I became less important than his obsession with pleasing his uncle. I hoped my husband would be willing to fight for me again."

"Fight who?" Bliss asked. "Your lover wouldn't be Roger Cahnman, would he?"

"You really are clever, aren't you? How long have you known?"

"Not until now. I should have guessed before. The way you reacted when I thought I saw him in the garden . . . and then again when I suggested he and Melody were a couple," Bliss said. "Osmond must have learned the truth. That's why he got into that fistfight with Roger."

Bliss moved in a small arc toward the camera, forcing Hope to turn with her. Logan's mouth went dry. He knew exactly what she was trying to do—to give whoever was watching a clearer view of Hope—but if she saw the tally light . . .

That was it! Logan raced back through master control.

"Hey, boss! What's going on?" Vern asked.

"Call the police. Tell them to get here right away."

Over the monitors he heard Hope saying, "The old hypocrite fired Roger." Her voice rose. "I told him I would get a divorce. Osmond said he would make sure I wouldn't get a dime since everything but modest salaries belonged to the ministry. Roger didn't have savings or a great background, either. I was afraid to be poor again, so I stayed. That sanctimonious old preacher made life even more of a hell . . ."

Logan lost some of the dialogue as he ran down the hall and quietly entered the backstage area. But as he drew closer in the dark, he picked up on Hope once more.

" . . . but from now on Roger and I will be together, living on Osmond's money, knowing that he'll keep on paying in other ways. We'll simply disappear and be satisfied seeing Osmond Wright in disgrace because of financial and moral misconduct."

Logan frowned as he skirted the flat and got into position behind Hope. Moral misconduct? Had Osmond been having an affair with Melody, after all? The reason for blackmail didn't matter now. He had to disarm Hope before she killed the woman he loved.

EVERYTHING but where her sister fit into the picture was
falling neatly into place for Bliss.

"You were so clever using the Bible to write the blackmail notes," she told Hope. "Why do you think Osmond's congregation will care about something he did
thirty years ago."

"So you know," Hope said. "Who told you? Joelle?"

"Actually no one. Those dark eyes of Dean's should
have been a giveaway, but the black-and-white monitors
and photo made Dean's light red hair look silver and the
slight resemblance more pronounced. Of course, a
nephew could look like his uncle. But since Joelle is Lurlene's sister, there's no reason for the two men to look
alike at all." From Hope's amazed expression, Bliss knew
she'd ferreted out the truth. "Good reason for blackmail. How did *you* figure out Dean was Osmond's natural son?"

Hope's laugh was bitter. "Osmond had my mother-in-
law keep an eye on me these past weeks. His big mistake. Joelle might want to be loyal to him in spite of
everything, but when she drinks... We had reason to be
bitter together. She told me she still cared about him, that
she had dated Osmond first, but that he'd thought Lurlene would make a better minister's wife. Eventually I
worked the whole truth out of her."

Bliss was horrified when Logan stepped out from behind the flat. His expression clearly told her he'd heard
everything. Then a white-faced Hope whipped around
and pointed the gun at him. Her hand was shaking.

"Just stay right where you are."

"Or you'll what? You can put the gun down," Logan
told her. "You've just made a nationwide confession over
CLN."

Bliss didn't think Hope would shoot anyone purposely, but one never could predict accidents. She lunged for the larger woman and knocked her off balance.

"Bliss, let me handle this!" Logan yelled.

But she wasn't in a position or of a mind to take orders. She had her hands on the gun and was trying to pry it loose from Hope's desperate grip.

"Let go!" Hope shrilled.

Bliss pretended to acquiesce, then hit Hope with all her weight. The two women went flying to the ground, a tangle of hands and legs. The gun discharged, the sound echoing around the stage. Hope freaked out, screamed and loosened her grip. Bliss pounded at the other woman's hand with a fist and knocked the gun away. It went skittering across the studio floor.

Logan grabbed Hope, but it was obvious that the fight had gone out of her. Tears streamed down her face, but she didn't say a word. He let go and she curled forward into a tight ball where she sat.

"Bliss, are you all right?"

"Yes." Noticing movement, she turned as Dean stepped out of the audience and picked up the gun. He looked drawn and older than his years.

"Sorry that I let this go on so long. I'll take care of my wife now."

"You were here all along?" Logan queried.

When Dean nodded, Bliss asked, "What about my sister?" She grabbed the other woman's shoulder and shook it. "Hope, tell me you didn't hurt Melody."

"I didn't mean for anyone to be hurt," she cried. "But if I don't show with the money, I don't know what Roger will do."

"Oh, Lord," Bliss whispered, bounding to her feet. "I've got to go to her before it's too late."

"Not without me." Logan grabbed on to her arm. "But first I want Dean to answer a few questions."

"Logan," Dean said, as if reading his brother's mind, "Osmond told me everything after receiving the demand for money. Funny, but I wasn't really surprised. Somehow I think I already knew. But this can wait. Melody can't. Osmond is on his way to her at the Lord is My Shepherd Motel. We didn't know Roger would be waiting for him."

Logan reacted immediately. He pulled Bliss toward the aisle.

"Come on, Hope, get up," Dean murmured kindly. "It's over."

"No, it isn't!" she cried in a burst of defiance. "Osmond stole a million dollars from the ministry treasury."

"You didn't check the case very well. There's a few thousand on top, but the rest is cut newspaper."

Bliss glanced over her shoulder as Logan opened the door. Dean was stroking his wife's hair. Perhaps he did still love her, after all. But it was too late. Too late for Hope. Too late for her. The only reason Logan was so frantic to get to the motel was because of his father.

He had to protect Osmond at all costs. No doubt he would agree to stay in Wrightville. And she would go back to Indianapolis. Bliss and Melody. It had always come down to the two of them, together. It was one relationship they could both count on.

They drove silently through the night, everything around them a blur. Bliss glanced at the speedometer. The needle was pinned to the right. But she was too worried about her sister to protest, too numb to feel anything when Logan took a shortcut down a gravel road.

Soon she and Melody would be together again. That was all that mattered.

MELODY SHIVERED as she tried to steady herself in the bathroom doorway. The coolness of the night was seeping through her bones. The motel room was unheated and Roger was holding out a sleazy little outfit that he expected her to put on. In his other hand, he held a gun.

"What are you going to do to me?"

"We're waiting for Osmond to 'save' you, Melody."

He threw the outfit on the bed. Never letting the gun down, he made himself comfortable in a chair and propped up his feet on the bed.

"But why is a gun necessary?"

Melody could hardly focus on the weapon. It kept moving back and forth. She squinted and concentrated, but that didn't help. Her vision was blurred and she could hardly stand upright. Her mouth was dry, too. Roger must have drugged her food again. He'd done that yesterday, when he'd moved her from the trailer to this awful place. But Osmond would save her. Roger said so. And she remembered writing the note. But something was wrong. She was so confused.

Trying to focus on him, she asked, "Why did you make me write that note to Osmond?"

"Sweet revenge. Now make yourself beautiful, worthy of your minister." He flashed the gun toward the outfit on the bed.

"I don't want to wear that." Tears trickled down her cheeks. She wouldn't do what he said, not this time. "No."

"Sweetheart, you have a choice. Either put it on or I'll shoot you and frame Osmond for murder."

Melody swayed forward and made two attempts to snatch the thing up before she succeeded. She didn't want to die, so she had to do it. Osmond would forgive her.

"I'll change in the bathroom."

"Right here. You might pass out and I don't feel like exerting myself."

He waved the gun again and turned his back on her to look out the window.

"Yeah, I'll leave you here, nice and cozy, on the bed," Roger said. "I only wish I could be here for the big reception."

She was having trouble undressing. "You're leaving?"

"I have to, but don't worry, someone else will take over for me," Roger said, his back still to her. "He'll make sure you do what you're supposed to. If you don't cooperate, you'll force me to hurt Bliss."

Melody's head cleared a little at the mention of her sister. "Bliss is here?" she asked.

"Don't sound so hopeful. I've kept her from finding out where you are."

She pulled on the outfit. The room was starting to spin. She couldn't stay on her feet. Crawling onto the bed, Melody told herself she had to stay awake. She had to cooperate or Roger would hurt Bliss.

Gathering her faith around her as a cloak against the evil being perpetrated that night, Melody prayed for strength.

LOGAN ACCELERATED THE CAR and shot like a bullet through the night. Too many thoughts were crowding his mind, vying for his attention.

Dean his brother. He didn't know whether or not to be glad. But why hadn't he known?

Melody and his father, pawns of Hope and Roger's warped scheme. Were they merely in danger of scandal or of losing their very lives?

Bliss, so still and quiet beside him. She'd recognized the danger. Would she ever forgive him if anything happened to her sister?

Would he forgive himself?

He almost missed the turn. A sharp, fast left made Bliss fall toward him. Without a word, she slid back to her side of the car and clung to the door. A lump formed in Logan's throat as he thought about the possibility of losing her.

A pink-and-green neon sign blinked off and on ahead, heralding the Lord is My Shepherd Motel, a sprawling, one-story affair that needed more than a paint job to make it look inviting. He screeched into the far end of the lot in the nick of time. His father had just abandoned his own car closer to the rooms and was looking at the numbers on the doors.

"Stay here," Logan said.

But Bliss was already flying out of the car before he could put it in neutral. "The hell I will."

He didn't argue. He didn't know why he bothered to give her an order he knew she wouldn't take. At least they'd broken the silence.

She was already running toward his father. "Osmond, get out of here!" she yelled.

Logan sprinted to catch up with her as his father seemed about to enter a room anyway.

"I can't leave, Bliss. A young woman is in trouble and needs my help. I can't abandon her."

"Melody is my sister. I'll take care of her. This is a setup. Go, before it's too late!"

"She's right, Father." Logan slowed as he caught up to them. "Hope and Roger were working together. Dean is with his wife, but Roger may be in there now, waiting for you."

"No, Roger is right here."

Logan whirled around to find his former lighting director a few yards behind, gun in hand. Unlike Hope, Roger looked willing to use the weapon. Before it was too late to act, Logan inched toward him, hands spread wide in a conciliatory gesture.

"Roger, we don't want a big scandal. All this can be straightened out without anyone getting hurt."

"Stop right there."

Logan did as he said with only a few feet between them. He kept his eye on the weapon. The demon's hand was too steady for comfort. Sizing up the situation, he knew the other man had the advantage of height, weight and muscle. But Logan had desperation on his side.

"It's over, Roger. We know everything. Hope confessed. There's not going to be any money."

"I gathered that. But I can still get some reward by seeing that the preacher takes the fall Hope had planned for him."

"By using my sister?"

Logan turned toward Bliss, her face illuminated by blinking green and pink neon. She knew what he had to do—he could read the awareness in her eyes. And before

Roger could issue another order, Logan took a backward tumble onto the pavement and rolled against the villain's legs, knocking him off balance.

Down on his knees, Roger swung out with his gun hand and Logan felt his neck snap as steel came into contact with his jaw. He kicked out blindly and caught the other man in the side. Roger doubled up and Logan grabbed his right wrist, banging the gun hard against a support post. The weapon went flying just as vehicles began pulling into the lot.

Excited voices surrounded them.

Sirens wailed in the distance.

None of that stopped Roger who by now had grown desperate to get away. He kicked Logan in the jaw, then got to his feet. Although Logan didn't think he had it in him, he scrambled up. Catching Roger by the shirt back, he swung the man around and into the side of the building.

Roger grabbed his shoulder where Bliss must have wounded him in the pool house and sank to his knees in agony.

"Hey, what's going on here?" a woman asked, starting a string of questions delivered by a chorus of strange voices.

"Isn't that Osmond Wright?"

"Heath, is that the woman you told us about?"

Reporters and photographers. With flashes going off in his eyes, Logan scanned the people lined up for a view of the action. Arden Heath stood at the forefront.

"That's the Jezebel's sister," the fire-and-brimstone preacher intoned as he pointed to Bliss. "The silver-haired, silver-tongued devil is involved with both sisters."

Sure that she would try to attack the man, Logan moved to prevent it. Sirens wailed loudly as police cars pulled into the lot. His father stood tall and straight in the path, ready to take on Heath.

But the woman he loved was nowhere to be found.

"MELODY?" Locking the door behind her, Bliss rushed to the still figure on the bed. Fear of the unknown consumed her.

"Mmm." Melody's head turned and slowly her eyes opened. "Bliss? Am I dreaming again."

"No. You're not dreaming." She leaned over, stroked her sister's forehead and kissed her cheek. "I'm really here."

Melody pushed at her ineffectually. "Get away. He'll hurt you."

"Roger?" Bliss captured her sister's hands. "No, he's not going to hurt me, or you. Logan took care of him and the police are here now."

Melody wet her lips. "Osmond...?"

"He's all right, too. I'm going to get you some water." Bliss ran to the bathroom where she found a glass and filled it from the tap. A moment later she was back at her sister's side. "Can you sit up to drink?" She put an arm under Melody's back and helped her. When her sister had emptied the glass, she asked, "What did he do to you?"

"He drugged my food. I'll be okay." She looked around with a frown. "The stuff's already wearing off. My clothes."

"You take it easy. Take as long as you want."

"Now." She grabbed the skimpy top. "I hate this."

A pounding at the door made them both start. "Bliss, are you in there?"

"Yes."

"Is Melody all right? Let me in."

"Give us a minute," she called out. Then, in a soothing tone, she asked her sister, "Can you get dressed now?"

Melody nodded. Bliss gathered the clothes from the floor, then helped her sister change.

"Roger is an awful man," she said.

"Did he . . . hurt you?"

Their eyes met and Bliss's heart stopped for a moment.

But Melody assured her, "No, not like that. He embarrassed me and made me feel awful, but he didn't touch me."

"Thank God," Bliss whispered. She pulled her younger sister into her arms.

Melody explained, "He had Hope for that. She believes Roger loves her, but he doesn't."

Love. Bliss was beginning to hate the word.

She stroked her sister's hair. "Just forget all about them and what they tried to do to you. You won't ever have to think about it again. When we get back to Indianapolis—"

"No." Melody pulled out of the sisterly embrace. "I'm not going back. I found real love here."

Bliss averted Melody's eyes. "Logan."

"He's a friend."

"Osmond?"

"Not a man. I mean, not that way."

"Then what do you mean?"

"My faith. My love for Jesus," Melody told her. "He's brought me inner peace. And there's the ministry. It feels good to be needed."

"I've always needed you."

"And I'll always need you. But I can't depend on you for the rest of my life. I can't keep asking you to come to my rescue. I found something special here. I'm going to stay."

"I'm glad for you."

She *was* happy for her sister, though Bliss was sad for herself. Melody had the ministry...while she had no one. No, that wasn't true. She had herself. A person she could rely on. Why did the thought sound so unfulfilled?

"Let's get out of here."

Melody leaned on her as they made their way across the room. The sounds from outside intruded. As they approached the door, she said, "I love you, Bliss. I wish I could repay you for everything."

"You can repay me by being happy."

They hugged each other tightly and left the room. Flashes blinded Bliss as she tried to protect her sister from the photographers. Logan was waiting, along with a police officer who was keeping the reporters at bay. And Arden Heath was in handcuffs, being led to a squad car.

"I'll have my revenge on you yet, Osmond Wright!" the fire-and-brimstone preacher shouted. "You won't ruin my life twice and get away with it."

"He was part of the plot?" Bliss asked in surprise.

"From the very beginning," Logan agreed. "Hope involved him. Those sermons were leading up to tonight's performance."

A reporter interrupted. "What's the young lady's name?"

"If you want a story," Osmond said loudly, "I'll give you one. I have a confession to make to my congregation, something that I should have done thirty years ago."

Bliss felt a moment of gratitude and respect for the man. He was trying to protect Melody for the second time that night. If only Dean could have been saved from torment, this horror would never have happened.

Logan placed himself at Melody's free side. "The paramedics just arrived. They're going to take you to a hospital. We don't know what kind of drug Roger gave you . . . or if there will be any side effects."

They walked her to the ambulance where the paramedics helped Melody inside.

"I'm going with my sister," Bliss said. She was almost disappointed when Logan didn't argue.

He looked from her to his father. "I'll see you later."

She climbed into the ambulance and looked out the window. Logan was already on his way to Osmond. Obviously he thought his father needed him more than she did.

What else had she expected?


LOGAN WAS OUT OF PATIENCE by the time the reporters tired of their questions and left. Yet now that he had his father alone with the chance to get some answers, he wasn't sure how to begin.

Osmond leaned on the car next to his son. "Do you hate me?"

"I feel betrayed. You didn't tell me about the threats. You didn't tell me about a lot of things."

"Dean," Osmond said softly.

Logan couldn't figure out how he'd been too blind to see the truth he'd lived with for so many years. "You cheated me out of a brother."

"Lurlene would only allow Joelle and Dean to come live with us if I kept up the pretense."

"Mother knew? For how long?"

"Since Joelle found out she was pregnant. I know this is difficult for you to understand...but I fell in love with Joelle the moment I met her. She was so beautiful, so vibrant. But she wasn't the right partner for a minister. Lurlene was."

"You loved Aunt Joelle, but you married my mother?"

"I loved them both, if in different ways. It was a terrible choice for a young man to make, but I thought I was doing the right thing. And I did."

"Was it the right thing to get Aunt Joelle pregnant?"

"No, Logan, that was my sin." Osmond paused for a moment. "That was the first and last time. Just once, we turned to each other in weakness, and we've both regretted it since. I won't try to excuse myself. The guilt is part of my life."

"It's not me you have to convince, but Dean!" Logan said angrily. "No, that's not true. You're not what I thought you were. I believed in you. I've defended you! All these years you lived a lie. By cheating Dean, you turned him against me."

"I'm human, son. I've made mistakes, and have paid mightily by denying my own flesh. But the ministry will survive this scandal. When the furor dies, we will rebuild together."

"Don't include me in your plans."

"Not you. Dean. He's suffered most from my sin."

"He'll forgive you. He loves you, Father." Logan felt his throat constrict. "As I do."

"Thank you for that. I wouldn't listen to your mother when she tried to make me let go. I've put her through so much. Joelle and Dean. Bringing Heath before the church..."

"Mother didn't want you to do that. I remember."

"Joelle and Dean had just come to live with us and she didn't see how I could call Heath on moral grounds. But the circumstances justified what I did. Lurlene knew that, but she was afraid. Your mother has always tried to protect you."

Logan wondered what it would be like to share his father's love with Dean. Probably no different. Clearly Osmond was a man torn by circumstances, but one who loved both of his sons. It might take time, but he would come to terms with his disappointment in his father.

BLISS FELT THE RUSH of warm air against her neck and brushed a hand back to chase it away. Her fingers met warm flesh and hard teeth and she was startled wide awake. It took a moment to orient herself. She was in an uncomfortable hospital-waiting room chair, it was still dark and Logan sat next to her. She hadn't believed she would see him there.

"I have a feeling you're still angry with me." When she didn't answer, he added, "The silent treatment, huh? Maybe I'll get to say what I want without interruption for once."

"If you think you can—"

"I knew it was too good to be true."

Bliss shrank into her seat, crossed her arms over her chest and was determined to keep silent. He would make her crazy, make her feel things she didn't want to.

"My father and I had a few things to discuss. You might be surprised to know that he thought Gregory was responsible for the missing money and the blackmail because of an old gambling habit. Father figured he had gotten himself in debt again and had been dipping into the treasury. He wanted to give the man a chance to see the error of his ways and make restitution."

Unable to help herself, Bliss asked, "What about the phone call?"

"Father thinks that was one of our suppliers. The guy thinks sounding tough is an effective sales technique. According to Gregory, Hope had been draining the treasury a little at a time, probably since she realized the marriage didn't have a chance. By the way, Father is going to name Dean his successor."

"About time."

"I thought you would be pleased. So do you think I'll like living in Indianapolis?" he asked, startling her. "I don't suppose I'll have any trouble finding work there."

An odd feeling washing through her, Bliss whispered, "What are you talking about?"

"I like big cities, but I would rather have a home on a good piece of land surrounded by trees. And maybe a pond. A place similar to the one I have now, only bigger. Think we can find something like that within commuting distance?"

"What do you mean, *we*?" She hated the way her pulse was pounding, out of control.

"We as in you and me. A couple," he stated, confirming that he did mean exactly what she'd been afraid to assume. "Unless you're going to stay angry with me forever."

Forever was a long time, an amount she could imagine spending with him. But she was afraid to hope. He had other loyalties.

"Are you sure you won't want to come back to Wrightville?"

"I hope we'll be visiting on a regular basis," Logan said in a reasonable tone. "Maybe once a month in addition to birthdays, holidays, that sort of thing. I have a new brother to get acquainted with, after all."

A lump settled square in the middle of her throat. He had just learned he had a brother. She hadn't been thinking about his feelings.

"And I have a sister to visit," she added in a small voice.

"Is that a yes?"

"You haven't asked me a question."

"Will you marry me?"

Her heart began to pound in earnest. "Marriage won't be easy—"

"Don't start. Yes or no."

Bliss closed her eyes tight and prayed she wasn't making a mistake. "Yes."

"Then let's get out of here and celebrate."

"I can't."

"I've already checked on Melody," Logan assured her. "She's fine."

"I know."

"We'll be back to bring her home when she's released."

"That's not the problem."

"Then what is?"

"I can't go anywhere to celebrate because I don't have any shoes." Bliss stuck out her bare feet, which were scraped and filthy. "I left them in the studio."

"You're going to have to buy shoes that tie up. In the meantime, we can celebrate at my place. You won't need shoes—or anything."

Laughing, Logan rose and lifted her into his arms.

"What are you doing?" she cried.

"Using the most effective way I know to keep your mouth shut," he said, covering it with his own.

Bliss gave up. What use was there in arguing with a hardheaded man anyway? Besides, she had plenty of time.

A whole lifetime.

# Harlequin Regency Romance™

---

## Romance the way it was *always* meant to be!

The time is 1811, when a Regent Prince rules the empire. The place is London, the glittering capital where rakish dukes and dazzling debutantes scheme and flirt in a dangerously exciting game. Where marriage is the passport to wealth and power, yet every girl hopes secretly for love....

Welcome to Harlequin Regency Romance where reading is an adventure and romance is *not* just a thing of the past! Two delightful books a month, beginning May '89.

Available wherever Harlequin Books are sold.

# ANNOUNCING . . .

# *The Lost Moon Flower*
### *by Bethany Campbell*

Look for it this August
wherever Harlequins are sold

HR 3000-1

# *Harlequin Intrigue®*

# COMING NEXT MONTH

**#115 PHANTOM FILLY by Caroline Burnes**
The prize stallion from Dancing Water Ranch was missing, and the mysteriously sent video was the first clue in three years that Speed Dancer might still be alive. Trainer Dawn Markey was determined to get him back, even when the trail led cross-country. Even when her path crossed with breeder Luke O'Neil. Even when Luke became more than an ally. And even when it became clear that she was putting her very life in danger.

**#116 ROSES OF CONSTANT by Bethany Campbell**
Some kind of madness had overtaken the town. People lied under oath, planted evidence, made threatening phone calls. Unless Valery Essex got to the heart of the madness she would be convicted of murdering her husband and be separated forever from her little boy. Valery counted on Nikolas Grady, a newcomer who swore to uncover the conspiracy. But in a town of evil, even Nikolas was not what he seemed.

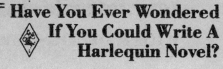

# Have You Ever Wondered If You Could Write A Harlequin Novel?

**Here's great news—Harlequin is offering a series of cassette tapes to help you do just that. Written by Harlequin editors, these tapes give practical advice on how to make your characters—and your story— come alive. There's a tape for each contemporary romance series Harlequin publishes.**

**Mail order only**

**All sales final**

------------------------------------------------------------

# Your favorite stories with a brand-new look!!

**H A R L E Q U I N**
*American Romance*®

Beginning next month, the four American Romance titles will feature a new, contemporary and sophisticated cover design. As always, each story will be a terrific romance with mature characters and a realistic plot that is uniquely North American in flavor and appeal.

Watch your bookshelves for a **bold** look!